THE BOOK OF FATES

SHADOW'S RISE

A NOVEL

ZENITH WOLFE

BAD APPLE

Los Angeles

Published by Good Ink, Los Angeles,
California.

ISBN 978-0-9989231-9-2

CHAPTER ONE

WHEN CURSES ARRIVE, THEY DO NOT KNOCK—THEY ENTER.

The Lightwices had been ordinary once. Or so their cul-de-sac believed.

They lived in a neighborhood caught somewhere between memory and make-believe—manicured lawns, golden retrievers, and weekend barbecues that felt just a little too storybook to be real.

In summer the air smelled of cut grass and lemonade—yet beneath it lingered something metallic, like iron on the tongue. On full-moon nights, the wind bent down their street as if whispering secrets to the trees.

At the center stood the Lightwice home.

From the sidewalk, it was flawless: lavender in perfect rows, a fence that never chipped, curtains glowing gold at dusk. Sprinklers hissed. A hand-painted mailbox grinned at the curb.

Perfect. Too perfect. Ordinary to the point of suspicion.

In Lee, Massachusetts—a postcard town that pretended nothing ever changed—curiosity wasn't a virtue. It was a liability.

Because inside that postcard frame, something old stirred in the bones of the house—something that beat like a hidden heart, patient and unyielding.

The Lightwices lived like time bent around them. Routines never faltered.

They never missed a town meeting. Not once in ten generations.

And yet no one remembered their faces changing—no lines deepening, no hair graying.

Neighbors forgot. Visitors lost track.

As if time itself had blurred them, wrapped in a forgetting spell no one could prove and everyone half-believed.

The Lightwices looked like an ideal family. Yet the veil of perfection was thin as glass.

And veils? They always crack.

What seeped through that fracture became an inheritance.

Some families pass down fortunes. Others pass down scars. The Lightwices inherited neither.

Their legacy was a curse—stitched from ancient oaths, haunted by monsters wearing the faces of those once loved. It clung to their name like frost on a grave marker: patient as winter, unwilling to fade.

They tried to ignore it.

Report cards taped up like trophies. Laughter rose from board games. Waffles stacked high in sunny kitchens. All of it borrowed joy—against a debt that was due.

And the house, patient, learned the rhythm of the curse.

The kitchen clock lost six minutes and would not return them. A framed photo tilted from the light.

Someone dreamed of a door with no handle and woke up tasting smoke.

Someone else set a place at the table without knowing why—until the chair scraped, though no one sat.

At first, the family called them coincidences. Then omens. Then nothing at all.

But shadows don't stay shadows. Given time, they sharpen into secrets. And the Lightwice's whispers grew teeth.

Still, the family did what families do: lit candles, opened windows, laughed louder.

But preservation does not last forever. And change was coming.

Not as whispers, but with a storm—one that would sweep over the town and break hardest on the two people the family had lied to the most.

Their daughters.

CHAPTER TWO

THREE DAYS BEFORE HALLOWEEN

It began on an October evening, a few nights before Halloween. The air carried cinnamon and burning leaves—sweet at the edges, bitter at the core.

Then came the silence.No ordinary stillness, but a heaviness like a never-ending waiting room in the pit of hell. Even the usual honks and chatter of Main Street had vanished beneath the hush.

And then—the storm arrived.

It started with a low moan, long and unbroken—the sound of something that had finally found what it was seeking.

Rain fell in punishing drops, slapping the earth like it wanted in. The clouds churned green-gray, the color of spoiled milk left too long in the sun.

Lightning spidered across the sky, but only above the Lightwice house, never beyond its shingles.

The neighbors noticed.

Some swore the air split open, a portal yawning wide, the roof peeled back like a wig in high wind. Others stopped asking questions altogether.

After that night, the Lightwices drew the curtains, dimmed the lights.

Swapped bulbs for candles. Draped velvet over windows.

They didn't vanish. They tried to disappear. But magic never slept.

Sprigs of rosemary turned up on porches—for luck.

Bundles of lavender and sage appeared on doormats—for protection.

White feathers drifted across sidewalks like whispered messages—carrying hope, love, or both, for star-crossed lovers.

These weren't displays of power. They were rituals.

Quiet. Deliberate. Ancient.

For generations, secrecy had been the Lightwices' strongest shield. Their magic was guarded so fiercely it hardened into legend—even within their own home.

Some relatives stayed as clueless as the neighbors mowing their lawns next door.

But secrets, no matter how deeply buried, always claw back to the surface. Some return as gossip. Others return as ghosts.

In Lightwices' case, they returned as a curse.

It hadn't begun with them.

Yet one way or another—it would end with them.

CHAPTER THREE

THREE DAYS BEFORE HALLOWEEN

Riya and Haley Lightwice—cousins, best friends, born on the same Halloween night—had no idea their lives were built on centuries of magic and lies.

No clue they were living on a fuse waiting to be lit. They were fifteen, almost sixteen—three days to go.

Their biggest worries? Homework, hallway gossip, and finding the perfect thrifted sweater before someone else snagged it.

They could've passed for sisters—maybe even twins if the light hit just right.

Wild spirals of curls framed their faces like halos. Their mixed heritage shimmered in every feature: deep brown eyes lit with equal parts mischief and wonder, and skin kissed by two continents—smooth, sun-warmed, and glowing like dark honey.

Their moms, Celeste and Raven Lightwice, were fraternal twins with irresistible appeal.

Celeste, with her sleek dark hair and porcelain skin, had a calm, crystalline presence. Raven, all dark auburn edges and cream-toned sharpness, carried the fire.

Together, they radiated the kind of offbeat charm that made people linger a little too long in their downtown shop, *Star Struck*.

Part vintage boutique, part old-book haven, part crystal-infused magic den, the store was a kaleidoscope of intention for anyone trying to find themselves, or at least accessorize the journey.

Their dads, Xavier and Manchester Garlock, were brothers—doctors bound not just by blood, but by heritage, wisdom, and humor forged in experience.

Both had skin like ultraviolet obsidian and hair coiled tight with power. One spoke like thunder, the other liked jazz, but both moved with the gravity of protectors.

That made Riya and Haley more than cousins. They were soul-bound—by legacy, by history, by something deeper still. Most days, they were normal. Well, mostly.

They dodged drama in the school hallways. Practiced varsity tennis. Made trades in the cafeteria like candy brokers on Wall Street.

And the town? The town had begun to change.

Pumpkins multiplied overnight. Bats made of black paper flew from every corner of the ceiling. Jack-o'-lanterns smiled with teeth that were too sharp.

But something had shifted. The fog clung too thickly. This Halloween felt... off. Worse—this year, their parents hadn't decorated.

Not a single fall wreath. Not one glowing witch hat. Just silence—like even the wind had forgotten how to play.

As the cousins crunched their way home through leaf-strewn streets, Riya broke the silence—as she so often did.

"Do you think they forgot?" she asked, her voice small, barely more than a whisper tucked beneath the collar of her jacket. "You know... to decorate... because of the weird storm over our houses?"

A garbage truck thundered by, drowning out her last few words.

Haley squinted, trying to catch them, but only saw Riya's apple-sized face disappear behind a cloud of worry.

Haley kicked a pine cone like it owed her money and shrugged.

"Maybe they're letting us handle it this year," she said, all cool and casual. "Teen independence. Trial by storm, literally."

She flashed Riya a crooked grin, the kind that dared the universe to try something.

Riya frowned.

"That's like giving up ice cream. Completely unnatural."

Their laughter faded as the air around them shifted—cooler, heavier—and the conversation died entirely when they nearly collided with their neighbors, Audrey and Sarah Malum.

Once childhood besties. Now, high school royalty turned sister ice queens.

Audrey flicked her paper-thin platinum hair. "Ugh, Riya. Careful—you nearly vibe-slapped me into next week!"

Sarah giggled, looping her arm through her sister's. "You two dressing up this year? Or are you just going as, like, sad DIY flops again?"

Haley grinned.

"You'll see. We're about to level up."

Audrey scoffed. "Don't forget to decorate. Fingers crossed it's not as tragic as your moms' 'witchy chic' fits."

The laughter trailed behind them like glitter-scented poison.

Back home, the cousins stood on Haley's porch—right next door to Riya's house—glaring across the street at the Malums' house, where their lawn exploded with perfect pumpkins.

"I wanna squash every smug gourd in that stupid display," Haley muttered.

"Tempting," Riya said. "Still technically illegal."

They slipped inside.

The house was warm, cinnamon-coffee-scented, and laced with the low murmur of voices.

Their parents were already home—too early, too calm.

Riya didn't say a word, but a grim little plan began to take shape.

CHAPTER FOUR

THREE DAYS BEFORE HALLOWEEN

"Heyyy," Riya called, eyes wide with exaggerated cheer. "Sooo, Haley and I were thinking... maybe this year you skip the haunted-doll costumes and try something normal?"

She flinched as her mom—Celeste—turned.

The movement was deliberate, spine curling like a cat about to pounce, each vertebra unfolding in quiet threat. Her eyes narrowed to slits.

Riya flinched—but pressed on, her voice dropping to almost a whisper.

"Like, I dunno... cat ears? Angel wings? Something basic but still cute?"

Celeste squared her petite shoulders and raised one perfectly arched eyebrow—the kind of look that could end arguments or start revolutions.

Riya's heart thumped harder. That look—cool, calm, just a little dangerous—meant business. And worse? It looked exactly like her own.

"Well, hello to you, too," Celeste said, sipping her cream-loaded coffee with a smirk.

"Hi, Mom," Riya huffed, already annoyed. "Can you just... listen for a sec?"

"Mm-hmm. Listening. But cat ears and wings?" Celeste tilted her head. "Sweetie, the costumes we wear every year are for the Charmwic Ball.

You know, the one we've been going to every Halloween since before you could spell 'spooky.'"

Riya opened her mouth to argue, but Celeste kept going. "And, just so we're clear, I'm the older twin. Like you are with Haley. So naturally, I outrank you." She winked over her mug.

Classic Celeste.

Riya groaned. "People talk. It's... embarrassing."

A beat passed before Celeste flipped her brown hair—naturally frosted at the tips—over one shoulder. Her ivory skin flushed with irritation.

The Lightwice women ran the show. Always had.

It's why Riya and Haley carried their mother's surname and why Haley, though bold in most things, chose her words carefully.

"I'm down with weird," Haley said, flashing a disarming grin. "But Auntie Celeste, it was just... something we were talking about earlier—"

"Something what?"

The voice cut through the air like velvet-wrapped lightning. Haley didn't even have to turn.

"Mom," she said, trying to keep her smile from twitching, "Hi."

Raven swept in, trench coat black as midnight, boots clicking like punctuation. Her lipstick matched the cinnamon swirl in her coffee—warm, bold, dangerous. Her glare could melt steel—or at least freeze a baby deer mid-prance.

"Darling, if this is about last year's haunted doll look, you loved it. *Iconic but deeply unsettling*—your words."

"It *was* iconic," Haley backpedaled. "Just maybe... too iconic? Like, emotionally scarring for the neighborhood... kids."

Raven gave a delighted gasp. "Then it worked. A classic."

Celeste clinked her mug against Raven's thermos. "Cheers to that."

Riya groaned. "We never stood a chance."

"Not against this," Haley agreed, gesturing to their moms like they were their own Broadway production.

And honestly? They were.

"Okay, fine," Raven relented with a dramatic eye roll. "But don't you two want to start decorating for your big party? Or were you planning on the neighborhood kids doing it for you?"

Haley was just about to answer when Raven noticed her coffee cup was empty.

She twisted toward the pot, and her chestnut hair slipped to one side, falling like silk curtains drawn back from a stage.

There, at the base of her neck, the scar emerged—subtle but unmistakable.

A raised triangle, branded into existence, cradled three lines that fanned downward like the rays of a dying sun—all enclosed in a perfect circle.

The skin around it shimmered faintly, as if the mark still remembered its own burning.

It wasn't just a scar. It was a story, sealed in flesh—unfinished, still being

14

written.

No one knew exactly where the mark had come from. Raven never spoke of it. Not to Riya. Not to her daughter. Not even when the nightmares came.

Just like she never explained why one of her eyes had turned ice-blue while the other remained a warm, thoughtful brown.

The contrast was striking—like winter and spring trapped in the same stare.

Everyone in the family acted like it was no big deal. Like it was just another quirk in a house full of unexplained oddities.

But there were moments—when the moon hit just right or the wind shifted mid-sentence—when even silence felt like a warning.

When she returned, coffee steaming in hand, her tone shifted.

"Haley. Riya." Raven cleared her throat like she was about to declare a new family rule. "You two are officially on decoration duty. And yes, we're wearing the same costumes. And yes, we're going to the ball."

She took a loud, unapologetic sip of coffee—effectively ending any debate about costumes or balls for the next hundred years.

"No complaints. No take-backs. It's tradition, my loves."

Riya recoiled like she'd been slapped.

"Um, can you not do that?" she snapped, her voice rising over the strange ringing in her ears that always showed up when things got tense. She couldn't take another round of school teasing, especially not from Audrey and Sarah.

That's when her dad, Manchester, slowly swiveled his bar stool around—one elbow still resting on the counter, the other cradling a steaming mug of plain coffee, as if it might keep him from unleashing a whole monologue.

His sharp features—angular jaw, high cheekbones, and feline-cut eyes the color of storm-glass tucked in warm caramel skin—had a way of narrowing when he was serious.

And right now, they were locked on her like lasers.

Riya's throat went dry.

"Riya," he said sternly, "where is all this coming from? We've never heard you talk like this before."

"It's just... Audrey and Sarah are coming to our party. And basically the whole school," Riya muttered, barely holding it together. "We just wanna seem, I don't know—normal for once. Maybe even, like... not totally cringe."

Despite Manchester's academic mindset and professor voice, he was all softness beneath the surface. But tonight, even he looked shaken.

He stood, pressing his hands into his slacks—his default intimidating dad pose—flashing his dull gold wedding band like a badge.

"Look," he said gently, choosing each word like it might crack, "I don't think the costumes are the issue and—"

"BUT THEY ARE!" Riya burst out, the words hitting the air before she could shove them back in.

And that's when Haley's dad—Xavier—eight years younger than Manchester, a little more hoodie than hardcover—stepped in with the kind of calm that made her stop breathing.

His voice dropped. "One day, it'll make sense. But right now? You're not ready."

"Not ready for what?" Riya snapped. "The weird ball where everyone dresses like a cursed vintage catalog? Or are we just not ready to die of public humiliation?"

Silence.

Haley's eyes flicked to her dad, her brow tense.

The question lingered like static in the room, thick and sparking.

"So, what—we're just supposed to go along with whatever you say and never ask why?" she said, voice rising. Her cheeks flushed a stormy red. "That's the deal?"

"In a way, yes," Xavier said flatly.

That made things worse.

Mysterious family secrets? That was basically code for *yep, we're officially weird*.

Riya couldn't take it anymore. She cracked like a five-year-old sprinting through a Lego minefield.

"Just tell us why you're so obsessed with RUINING OUR LIVES!" she screamed. Her voice was wild like a swarm of cicadas shrieking into a summer night.

Then—SMACK. WHOOSH. WHAM.

Xavier's hand slammed the counter, sending a low rumble through the kitchen.

His long braids slipped across his face in a smooth S-curve, one strand flashing like onyx in the light. His hazel eyes—usually warm, creased with dad-joke grins—had gone dark. Stormy.

That made Riya's heart thud harder than she wanted it to.

"Enough!" he boomed. "You know we don't keep secrets in this family."

His voice filled the room. At six-foot-six, with muscles for days, he didn't need to shout, but when he did, it echoed.

"There will come a time when you'll know everything. Who you are... what we are. But for now, you have to trust us. Just do what we say and—"

"STOP!" Haley snapped, throwing up a hand like a traffic cop.

"Everyone's acting seriously weird. Ray and I just wanted to know if,

16

maybe this year, you'd ditch the estate-sale costumes and do something for us for a change."

She exhaled sharply, tilting her head in that way that made her look older than three days away from sixteen—tired, sharp, a little too aware. "Maybe we're asking for some classic selfishness. But... a family fight? Drama? Over costumes?"

Then she spun toward Riya in a flourish, her shoulder-length spirals frizzing and bouncing like punctuation.

"You know what?" she added, voice dripping sarcasm. "We're *sorry*, okay?" She glanced down, then back up. "Come on, Ray. Let's go."

She turned on her heel, muttering as she walked, "We love you, but this whole conversation is giving major cult energy."

Raven's eyes sparkled—like something had clicked—but Haley didn't have time to decode it.

Riya was already storming up the stairs like a girl on fire.

The middle step let out its usual whiny squeak, like two mice arguing under the floorboards.

"Ugh, seriously?!" Riya yelled. "Another thing we have ZERO control over! This creepy step!"

She bolted up the rest of the stairs. A second later, she flung herself face-first onto Haley's bed with a dramatic groan that could rival a dying animal.

"Do you think this ball thing is, like... some weird grown-up secret club or something?" Riya mumbled, practically tucked into her shoulders.

Haley snorted. "No. Our parents are way too boring for that."
She gave a half-cracked grin. "The weirdest thing they do is that broom superstition."

"Oh yeah!" Riya squeaked, sitting up. "The open-broom-moto. 'If a broom falls and nobody calls it—somebody's lying.' Creepy, but true."

"Yeah, well... no brooms fell," Haley said, kicking off her sneakers and pulling on her coziest pajamas.

The air between them hung quiet, thick with questions neither of them wanted to ask out loud.

"So... what do you think your dad meant?" Riya finally said, her voice barely above a whisper.

Haley didn't answer right away.

She just stared at the ceiling like it might crack open and give her the truth.

"I think this birthday's gonna change everything," she said at last, her words soft but sure, like she'd already seen it written in the stars.

They didn't know it yet, but outside, the wind had changed.

17

Something was coming.
Something old. Restless. Hungry. Watching.
It had waited long enough.

CHAPTER FIVE

THREE DAYS BEFORE HALLOWEEN

Of course, Riya and Haley weren't thinking about ancient bloodlines or fate-tangled curses.

Right now, it was full-blown teenage triage: flashcards, chemistry class, and the looming threat of throwing the lamest Halloween party in suburban history.

"Ugh, I'm so dead," Riya groaned, collapsing into her textbook like gravity had finally claimed its prize.

Haley shot up from the bed as if she'd just gulped down a pumpkin-spiced latte. "Not tonight, Ray. We've got three days to make this house scream Halloween."

Riya groaned into a pillow. "Can't we just recycle last year's costumes and toss out some off-brand candy?"

Haley spun on her heel. "Oh, cool, yeah, let's totally get roasted by Audrey and Sarah when they roll in looking like the Haunted Mansion styled them personally."

"They always show up like that."

"Exactly. That's why we need to bring the glam. Broom-core realness. Think—haunted and high fashion."

Riya sighed. "If I flunk chemistry because I was hanging a skeleton garland, I'm blaming you in my college essay."

Haley grinned. "Worth it. Besides, your GPA is powered by straight-up wizardry."

Haley was already halfway to the attic.

"Glitter boots and glory," she called over her shoulder. "Let's go."

Suddenly—*click-thump*—the attic ladder fell open with a creaky groan.

Less than a second later, the cousins stood in Haley's dusty loft, where the holiday decorations lived out their retirement in peace—dingy sheets draped over forgotten furniture like ghosts.

Crates and boxes labeled "Dishes" and "Old Books" cluttered the middle of the room, resembling a maze for mice.

The wood floor whimpered under their steps. The attic seemed to hold its breath, like it was listening.

"Do you think I woke them?" Riya whispered, pulling her knees up to her chest.

Haley scanned the room. "No, I don't think so... but—"

A *screeeech!* Sharp and shrill like a barn owl in distress or a violin being murdered ripped through the air.

Riya and Haley were too late.

Ten bulbous toads—longtime attic squatters—had stirred.

Their terrarium pulsed with soft light as the toads croaked in chaotic unison—like a drum line gone rogue. Their thick brows twitched in time with the noise, and their green skin ended in fingertips dipped brown, as if someone had dunked them in chocolate for no reason at all.

They were long-forgotten pets.

One—with a bent front toe and a resting face permanently stuck on "judgy"—had been dubbed Sir Grumpsby when the cousins were five. He still looked deeply unimpressed.

Riya and Haley had named them all from afar as kids, but never once held them in person.

That was the rule—strict orders from their parents.

Only the adults were allowed to handle the toads. It had always felt... weird. And yet, even now, they still obeyed.

Trying to ignore the chaos, Riya sat on a dusty swivel stool, swinging her legs while Haley dropped to her knees by a honey-stained trunk.

She rummaged through moth-chewed sweaters like a knight on a noble quest.

"Whatcha looking for?" Riya asked, raising an untamed eyebrow.

"Those red boots from Grandma Ama," said Haley. "I want to be—"

She stopped.

"Wait—ew, WHAT?!" Riya shrieked, snatching her hands back like the trunk was radioactive.

"I felt something...cold."

"Dude, are you trying to die?" Riya yelped, furiously scrubbing her hands on her sleep shirt like they were cursed.

Haley reached deeper and pulled out something much heavier than a pair of vintage boots.

It was a book.

And it was massive—easily the size of a school binder, though three times as thick and infinitely heavier.

It looked like it had been dragged through fire, buried beneath ash, and unearthed by something with unfinished business.

Over three hundred pages were bound in leather so dark and cracked that they resembled petrified wood. The edges were jagged, torn like a cursed saw.

Its scent lingered in the air: old smoke, scorched sugar, and something metallic beneath it.

The cover shimmered with a sheen that refused to stay still—black one moment, then bruised blue, then a shade of indigo that felt impossibly deep as if the book was reflecting not light, but absorbing it.

At its center blinked a single eye.

Set within a bulbous cradle of scarlet-stitched leather, the eye was unmistakably reptilian—glass-like, antique, and terrifying. Its pupil burned like a blade of molten amber, while the iris spiraled with galaxies.

It didn't just look at Riya and Haley. It felt like it remembered. It knew.

The longer Riya stared, the less certain she was of her own thoughts. The eye tugged at her mind, quiet but relentless, like invisible hands unwinding her from the inside.

A title began to surface. Letters in crumbling gold shimmered into view, then collapsed, then tried again—desperate to be read, yet barely able to hold themselves together.

The words shifted like a living spell.

The Book of Fates.

Haley didn't flinch. If anything, she leaned closer. Like the book had been waiting—not just to be found, but to be found by her.

Riya's breath hitched. Her chest tightened. It was like standing too close to a cliff that was also staring back.

Her jaw dropped. "Tell me that's just a really bougie diary," she said, backing up like the thing might sprout legs and ask for a blood pact.

Haley's voice barely rose above a breath. "It feels... alive."

She shifted her arms, trying to get a grip on it, but the book was too heavy, too slippery, as if it didn't want to be held. It slipped through her fingers and hit the floor with a deafening WHAM.

The attic toads lost their minds. Sir Grumpsby pressed his bulbous face to the glass, glaring in pure amphibian scorn. He sounded like a two-hundred-pound chicken in full meltdown.

Riya stumbled back and cracked her head on a beam.

BANG—and collapsed face-first—flat as roadkill.

The sound shut the toads up instantly. They curled into balls like sleepy lollipops, wiped their eyes with purple tongues, and drifted off like nothing happened.

Haley didn't budge. She was locked onto the book as if it were casting a spell.

Riya groaned, dragged herself up, and stomped over.

"Um—hello? I just got body-slammed by a... whatever it's called ... and you're over here getting married to a book?!"

Haley barely looked up.

"Sorry, Ray, but this book is... insane. It's freezing like a rock left in the snow and way heavier than it looks."

She ran her fingers along the cover, brow furrowed. "And the leather? It feels like... old skin or something."

Then her breath caught.

"Wait—look!"

She pointed near the top of the book, her voice dropping. "That mark... It's the same triangle-circle symbol on the back of my mom's neck."

Riya was drawn to something else entirely—a clasp at the book's edge, cool to the touch and carrying the faint tang of rust.

"That thing..." she whispered, fingertips grazing the worn bronze before knocking softly, like on a tiny door meant for a mouse.

"It's an ouroboros..."

A clawing sound tore from the snake-shaped lock as it uncoiled, tail slipping free like a ribbon that had waited too long to be opened.

Then—*snap!*

Pages fluttered wildly, golden light pulsing from the seams, like the thing was breathing... or waking up.

Riya and Haley stumbled back in sync and dropped the book.

On the first page, ink bled upward through the parchment, curling into letters that hadn't been there a heartbeat ago.

Words formed slowly, each one deliberate, as if the book were deciding what truths they were ready to hear.

Haley leaned in, her fingers gripping the edge of the pages as if she could anchor herself to the words. Riya pulled back, shoulders angling away, as though distance alone might soften whatever was about to be revealed.

The message that appeared in *The Book of Fates.* was something the cousins had never expected to see.

I am neither Light nor Shadow. Neither Good nor Evil. I take no side. I only remember.

All majick—Light and Shadow alike—dwells within me. And now... so do you.

Think of me as your cosmic companion—loyal, curious, perhaps a touch intense—but bound to you now, my Keepers.

That is your birthright. You cannot burn me. You cannot drown me. You cannot tear me apart. Not even the stars could erase me.

I was bound before time drew its first breath, sworn to an ancient pact— Divine and Abyssal, celestial and chthonic.

Only one force may unmake me, and only when the universe exhales its final breath.

Until then, I will answer when you ask. I will whisper what you crave into the silence. I can grant you peace. Or I can raise an empire of Shadow from the ashes of a thousand stolen powers.

What I become depends solely on you.

A long, wheezing exhale escaped the book.

"...Did it just sigh?" Riya asked, frozen mid-butterfly stretch. "Please tell me that was just me."

Haley's eyes narrowed. "It sounded like the book... was breathing."

Before either of them could react, the book flipped a page—on its own. They both jumped. The page stilled.

Then—slowly—letters began to shimmer into view. Faint at first, like whispers pressed into ink. Then brighter. Bolder.

A glittering script that pulsed as it danced across the parchment, alive with some ancient, unreadable rhythm. A whole paragraph scrawled itself out and then vanished.

Another page turned. More glowing script. Then gone. Again. And again.

The book was writing, deleting, and moving on—as if auditioning thoughts and erasing the ones that didn't stick.

"Whoa," Riya whispered, pushing up to her knees. "It writes... and deletes? That's not even possible."

But it was happening—letters blooming, vanishing, like the page was a garden of words.

Whatever this was, the cousins were not in control. There was no going back. Only forward.

From deep within the spine, something shifted—a sound like a sigh, or the slow turning of a key in a lock no one had touched in centuries.

And in that hush, it felt—impossible—as though the book had heard them.

Somewhere deep in its memory, as it drew its first breath in centuries, it was born anew — and in the exact moment, it was already writing its own end.

Their end.

CHAPTER SIX

THREE DAYS BEFORE HALLOWEEN

The one reaction Riya and Haley shared was the way finding the book made them both second-guess everything. What else lurked in their secret attic?

Until now, it had only been a place their parents searched when something lost needed finding—only to miraculously reappear up there, as if it had been waiting all along.

Even their grandparents had treated it as a last-ditch hiding spot, a maybe-it's-there-if-you-look sort of place. Come to think of it, everything lost was eventually found in that dusty loft.

It was, in its way, a mysterious space. One Riya and Haley had never lingered in. That was about to change. Actually, everything was about to change.

Because the book—with a final flutter—let its pages settle... and a fresh spread unfurled. No moving words this time. No vanishing sentences. Just a single paragraph.

A timeline—clean and simple, like a ballet barre with branching limbs. From each branch, memories bloomed like flowers in fast-forward.

Your parents crossed paths sixteen years past, on All Hallows' Eve—beneath the lantern light of the Charmwic Ball.

Riya, your parents have borne forty-five winters in ash years.

Haley, your mother counts forty-four; your father, thirty-seven in ash years.

    And not long after that night, you and Riya came forth into the world. Same hospital. Same day.
Two cries born under the same full moon.
Now, your sixteenth turning stands but days away.
This is no mere map. It is a memory. A warning. A beginning.
Do more than see it. Memorize it.

    A scratchy sound echoed like a quill dragging itself across ancient parchment.
    Ink bled through the page in slow, deliberate strokes.
    A map began to form.
    Spindly trees. A still, black pond. A narrow path wound behind their homes—the one Riya had never dared to follow. And at its end, scrawled in shimmering ink like a secret finally spoken:
    The Charmwic Ball.
    A faint breeze stirred, carrying the scent of smoke and sugared violets that had been left too close to a flame.
    From somewhere in the distance, music trembled through the air... and then was gone.

CHAPTER SEVEN

THREE DAYS BEFORE HALLOWEEN

Haley and Riya exchanged a look—wide-eyed, frozen, not breathing.

"Um... Hales," Riya whispered, voice wobbling like a roller skate with a busted wheel. "This is officially getting creepy."

She pointed to the back of the house, where shadows didn't just gather—they stacked, folding into each other until they looked solid, like a bruise spreading across the yard.

"That ball's never been behind our houses, right? I mean, we would've noticed a whole gothic estate. Unless it's, like... cloaked? Cursed? Both?"

She pinched her untamed brows.

"Listen to me," she groaned. "I sound all witchy-chic already. What's happening to me? To us? Oh, Hales... why me?"

Recognition crossed her face like a storm cloud dragging rain. A memory flickered—Celeste once whispering it was "the only dance worth dressing up for," before snapping the words shut like they'd escaped by mistake.

Now it didn't feel like a mistake at all.

Something was out there. And it had been waiting.

Then—snap!—the page split, spitting out a pop-up mini mansion in gleaming white, diamond staircase and all, its windows twinkling like constellations.

The tiny doors creaked open. White walls gleamed under glittering chandeliers. A miniature sign blinked to life, curling script spelling out: The Charmwic Ball.

Haley's eyes grew to the size of teacups.

"Okay, that's insane," she whispered, nudging Riya's leg. "Self-writing, pop-up book of doom? Guess my weekend plans just died."

Riya, meanwhile, had turned a lovely shade of panic-green.

"You know I hate surprises. And magic. And, uh, books that literally breathe," Riya muttered, eyes wide. "They're supposed to sit on shelves, not build mini haunted mansions."

"Ray," Haley said gently, her voice softer now. "Remember what my dad said? 'One day, you'll understand what you are?' Maybe... this is it."

Riya half-snorted. "Or maybe you've been breathing too much attic dust," she said, eyeing the book like it might suddenly ask for the Wi-Fi password. "No way this is real. It's gotta be a prank."

But even as she said it, the glow from the page pulsed again—soft, golden, and oddly... inviting.

It seemed to beckon them closer, like a warm breath against cold skin, promising answers they didn't know they craved.

Still trembling, the cousins leaned in and began to read more.

The Charmwic Ball is no mere gathering, but the once-yearly summons of all who bear majick's mark.

There, they pay homage to the Fates—the weavers of balance, keepers of Light and Shadow.

In the first breath of time, Light was born—and with it, Shadow.

When Shadow rose, Light did not yield.

Twins of the same cosmic cry: one to heal, one to defy. In ruin they battled, in stillness they remained.

Thus were the Fates bound to weave balance eternal—destinies measured, destinies entwined, until the end of all things.

And... with the first breath of time, a sacred place was born: the Light Veil—Sphalum.

Its name means crystal light, though no mortal tongue can hold its truth.

Sphalum is majick in its purest form—unbroken, untainted, shimmering as it did in the dawn of creation.

Picture twin orange suns, slow as turning pinwheels, casting their glow across a strawberry-milk sky that blushes seafoam green when it rains.

There is a town—small, familiar, almost like yours—yet stranger, lovelier. Its streets curl around a lake so clear it reflects not your face but your onu, your soul. That lake spills into a golden ocean, whose waves hum lullabies each time the moons rise.

And oh—the moons. There are three.

The stars hang heavy and low, so near that the bold can reach for them.

The reckless climb enchanted ladders, plucking them like fruit. Some keep the stars in glass jars to light their homes. Others set them adrift again, whispering wishes as their glow drifts skyward.

At the heart of it all reigns Queen Zion of Coelum—what mortals might call Heaven.

She does not wear a crown. She wears light itself and a loose white suit drifting like a cloud.

Mocha skin lit from within, as if she swallowed a star. Curls that coil and spiral like licorice caught in a storm.

Wherever she walks, the universe softens.

Her greatest treasure is a moonstone amulet—one that breathes the past, present, and future in a single vision.

Her greatest joy? Handing out Cricket Drops—candies that chirp the instant they're bitten. They taste of wildflowers, or lightning, or—on unruly days—pure mischief. She laughs as the majick folk guess their flavors, her smile widening with every wrong answer.

In Sphalum, peace is not suggestion but law.

Evil does not flourish there. It wilts. It shrinks. It burns away beneath the brightness, like paper beneath a magnifying glass.

But remember this: even the brightest light casts a shadow.

The book flipped again.

This time, dark smoke curled around the pages, and an inkblot formed like a drop of blood.

It spread into a haunting story.

Far beyond the edges of the known universe lies Dahmorte—the Shadow Veil.

Its name translates to death by war, and every misfortunate creature bound to this Veil has paid for eternity with their bone and blood.

The air bites. The sky screams. The earth scorches underfoot.

The only light? A swollen, purple moon that looms like it was dunked in grape soda and forgotten by time.

Queen Hexima rules there.

And yes, she is every bit as terrifying as she sounds.

Her lips are stained plum—her skin, waxy and pale.

Lavender eyes blaze like haunted headlights.

Her hair spirals into a stiff cone that swallows her oversized crown.

On a good day, she looks like a baby zombie on a throne of nightmares.

She has been imprisoned in Eldritch for a sentence older than time—a cursed forest where the trees lean in to listen, where their roots creep like slow-moving serpents, and ash drifts like snow from no fire that can be found.

The air tastes of iron and rotting eggs, and the ground remembers every footstep that dares cross it.

Eldritch feeds on those it holds, drinking their strength, stealing their onus, until even their shadows forget them.

The Rede—the oldest, wisest magic council—banished Queen Hexima there after she attacked the ashes (that is what the Veils call you: humans) and unleashed an energy-virus that nearly broke the world.

But Queen Hexima does not stay trapped for long.

She always finds a crack to slip through—usually with the help from her grotesque bodyguards—the Shiverskins.

Creatures wrapped in borrowed flesh, stitched from the remains of battlefields.

Their thorny teeth jet past scaly lips, always grinning, always hungry.

They wear their victims' faces like masks—loose, sagging things—and speak only in the last words those faces had ever uttered.

A death-echo in unison.

Loyal to a fault. Bound to her will. And utterly, horrifyingly devoted.

Even worse is Harshmoon—the ruler of Everbind, the no-man's-land between the Veils. He is part lion, part serpent, part bird... and entirely a nightmare.

Over seven feet tall and stitched together like evolution gave up halfway, though technically a Moonglade, a prisoner of Hexima, he has turned Everbind into his personal Shadow domain

The no-man's-land between the Veils—it is the place I come from—the limbo for everything and nothing in the universe.

A wasteland soaked in Maldrop—that nameless sorrow that breaks onus. Most ashes that fall into Everbind never crawl out.

But some do. Some wake up. Some find the Fates.

The ash preditas—lost human onus—wander in misery, hunted by Elementals.

These spectral parasites slip between the Veils, feeding on ashs' pain like emotional vampires.

They cause nightmares. Heartbreak. Car accidents. Anything they can feed on. You will smell them first—burnt candles, old regrets—If you do... run.

Be warned...

Read on with clear intentions.

What comes next cannot be undone. Queen Hexima knows her time is coming to an end. Because of you.

36

You are the protectors—the Warriors of the Fates. You alone can restore balance.

Yet you must choose: Light or Shadow.

Your bloodline stretches across centuries, rooted in majick older than your surname.

Long before your first breath, the Fates inscribed their marks upon you—one to ascend, one to bring ruin.

Which is which... remains unseen.

Riya and Haley Lightwice.

The choice is coming. And it will cost everything.

CHAPTER EIGHT

THREE DAYS BEFORE HALLOWEEN

Riya sucked in a breath that sounded like seasonal allergies having a full-blown meltdown.

"Nope. Nope. No way. We are *not* magical!" she yelped, voice cracking like a bad connection. Her ears went ten shades of betrayal.

"We're normal. We do homework. We eat cereal. We are aggressively, painfully grounded."

She jabbed a finger at the book. "This? This is someone else's mess. We are *not* the chosen ones. Hard pass."

But their names lingered for an extra beat—and then the book had already turned another page.

It wasn't done with them yet.

With a thunderous *WHAM*, it slammed shut—only to snap open again, as if moved by its own will.

Pages whipped past in a frantic blur, rustling like wings in a storm, until one halted, dead still. Fresh ink bled across the parchment, curling into letters that shimmered like starlight dipped in a warning.

The toads stirred. The attic door jumped and jiggled.

The air split open into two shimmering doorways—one gold, one violet. Both pulsed like heartbeats, tugging at them in uneven rhythms.

The book rustled, daring them to choose and scrawled the rules in bold, jagged script:

ONE STAYS. ONE GOES. YOU DECIDE WHO IS SACRIFICED.

Riya sat frozen.

"This thing can't be serious," she groaned. "We're five pages in and already taking tests? Rude. Sure, let's pick our nightmare before the cursed book even warms up."

Haley edged forward, her body taut, drawn to the doors as if a string had hooked her spine. She swayed, eyes wide, like she could tumble straight through and never resurface.

She gasped.

"Ray," she whispered, her voice trembling. "I just... saw something."

Her senses buzzed, sharp and wild, almost too much to hold. "We have to pick the Light Veil's door. Together. Or we're finished."

"What?!" Riya snapped. "Oh great—the book's brainwashing you already. Lodging its warped thoughts right into your head?"

"It's not a joke," Haley said, stark and steady.

The book began tapping the page like a ticking clock.

Riya felt the pressure rising, a vise around her chest.

A snap cracked the silence. Time was up.

The cousins locked eyes. In unison, they whispered, "The gold door."

It cracked open with an agonized creak. Inside was... perfect.

At first glance, it was dazzling. Baby rabbits bounded across grass that shimmered like emerald glass. Miniature horses tossed their manes—glinting like spun silver.

Winged creatures zipped past in laughter, scattering trails of golden dust that hung in the air like fireflies.

Every smile shone bright and true. Every sound hummed with harmony. Even the air itself glowed, alive, as if the door was breathing them in and welcoming them home.

Then—the golden door slammed shut.

The book shrieked to life, pages flapping furiously, line after line clawing across the parchment like a possessed typewriter.

So... you doubt you are majickal? Yet you are. Both of you. Deeply. Undeniably. Your bloodline stretches back more than five thousand years.

Yes—the gold door was chosen truly. You show promise. You are listening well.

Mark this: Dahmorte's moon burns violet. Where Light gathers, the Shadow Veil yawns wide.

The violet door is no passage, but a snare—a claiming. Step through it, and Shadow takes you.

Know this also: your grandmother, Ama, is a Light-Trapper. She lassos the stars themselves and weaves their fire into spell and song.

Your grandfather, Henry, is a Veilbreaker—he can open portals to any realm and free any prisoner.

Celeste weaves spells from sheer intention—her gift, Chemisource, bending reality at its root.

Raven carries the balance; her spirit can slip through Shadow and Light, casting out evil before it takes hold. She was born to Astroproject.

And your fathers? They are Hives—powerhouses of will and majick.

And like your family, you will learn.

I foretold this over a millennium ago: Two cousins, born on All Hallows' Eve. Like twins. Destined to save the Fates.

That time is now.

You have never known... for on the hour of your first breath, Queen Hexima laid her hand upon you and bound you with a Shadow spell—a curse that has walked beside you all your days.

Yet now that you have found me, the curse is cracking. You could not have opened me unless you were the ones.

The chosen.

And I am here to help you save the world.

Riya jerked back like a startled, fainting goat, then snapped upright, blinking hard.

"W-wait—did that creepy antique just say it's gonna help us save the w-world?" she stammered, voice climbing an octave. "Like... *us* us?"

Haley exhaled hard, fluttering the page. "It's probably just being dramatic."

"No, Hales. It's right there. Black and white."

The book quivered and resumed writing.

Yes, Riya.

I speak truly—you will save the world, with Haley at your side.

If the hour has not already passed you by. If you are not too late...

Riya squealed, jumping back. "SEE?! Can we please tell our moms now?!"

"Not yet, Ray," Haley said, hugging the book like a life raft. "We need to figure out what this actually means first."

"Ha—ley, I'm losing it over here..." Riya groaned, clutching her face like it might hold her sanity in place.

Haley's voice softened. "Don't you want to know why we're different? What my dad meant in the kitchen?"

41

Riya clicked her cheek, rolled her chocolate-colored eyes—twice for good measure—and let out a dramatic sigh.

"Is that a yes?" Haley asked, already smirking.

"...Fine," Riya muttered. "I guess I'm a little curious."

The book didn't wait. It kept going.

Your powers are the key to restoring the Fates.

Heed this warning—ignore it, and all will unravel. Your rightful gifts will return only when you complete your gloaming at Aetherion Academy.

Then, and only then, shall immortality be yours.

You will face what others fear to name—vile Elementals. Shiverskins, loyal to the bone and stinking of Shadow. Harshmoon. And Queen Hexima herself.

You will meet the Rede. Magic's High Council. Harsh. Judgy.

Led by Ms. Treewith, a sour-faced storm-summoner with the personality of a thundercloud.

Then Mr. Seacoal, big and loud like a crashing wave.

And finally, Ms. Haute—the veiled doctor who moves like morning mist and glows like moonlight on water. Serene. Untouchable. A whisper in majickal form.

They are powerful. But distant.

But remember: The Light is never gone. Even on the darkest days, the sky behind the clouds is still blue.

Your mission begins now. All Hallows' Eve is coming. That is when Queen Hexima will strike. When the Veils are thin... and her power peaks.

Avoid the forest behind your homes—the Weld. It is twisted. Cursed.

Queen Hexima's energy coils through it like smoke. It will pull you in if you are not careful.

Whatever you need—spells and protection—you will find it here in me. Yet first, you must know your origin, for it was forged in a curse to end all curses.

A curse that even now coils around you, waiting. If you do not embrace your fate and wake the powers that sleep within, it will not only end your story—it will write its own.

CHAPTER NINE

THREE DAYS BEFORE HALLOWEEN

Riya barely held back a scream.

Instead, her lips clamped shut, and she let out a deflated wheeze like a balloon giving up on life. She couldn't believe the book revealed that their moms... were witches.

The revelation hit her like a gut punch from the universe itself. Which meant—if the book wasn't lying—she and Haley might have powers.

Still, she needed way more than glowing pages and dramatic backstory to buy into all this.

Like—really? Her mom could manifest anything? And Haley's mom could teleport?

It sounded like fiction written during a sleep-deprived sugar high. But... there had been signs.

Like how Riya's mom could swoop in for a last-minute science project with zero prep—and somehow, Riya would still ace it.

Or how Haley's mom could be at their shop, Star Struck, and five minutes later show up across town at the coffee shop, sipping chai like she hadn't just broken the laws of physics.

Riya stared at the ceiling, letting it all sink in.

"Oh my stars," she groaned, flopping back. "Our parents are actual magical weirdos. Full-blown. Certified."

She wobbled toward Haley like a kitten left out in a storm, trying to find its way back inside.

"So it's true," she said, pacing, "our parents go to that ball every year because it's where they met. And those embarrassing costumes? Apparently tradition."

She threw up her small hands. "I mean, what else are they hiding?!"

Haley was too distracted to answer. Her brain was spinning for different reasons.

"Do you think that's why they're letting us have our birthday-slash-Halloween party at my place?" she asked. "So they can sneak off to that witch party?"

Riya didn't respond right away. She turned away like someone trying not to wake a snoring friend at a sleepover, then started pacing.

After what she'd just read, "normal" felt like slippery soap—impossible to grip no matter how hard she tried.

A knot tightened in her chest. She didn't ask for any of this. And if magic was real—if she was real—then everything she thought she knew about her life was a lie wrapped in glitter and chaos.

So, in that moment, Riya made a decision.

She'd keep it secret. The book. The powers. The strange static she felt whenever the Malum sisters got too close.

All of it.

If she buried it deep enough, maybe—just maybe—she could still pass for normal. Even if the truth was already starting to burn through her skin.

Haley watched her cousin silently freak out.

"Ray, you okay?" she asked gently.

"Um—yes—no—ugh!" Riya finally said. Then she leaned in, whispering, "Do you think the book's lying to us?"

"You mean... straight-up lying?" Haley whispered, inching closer like the truth might bite.

"Yeah," Riya whispered back. "I mean, c'mon. A purple moon? Our moms having magical powers and immortal? My mom being a Chem—i—source? Your mom teleporting?"

"Why would the book lie?" Haley shrugged. "Honestly? It kinda tracks. Our moms never age, shop's basically enchanted, and yeah... fine, I'm buying it. For now."

"But how does it know everything?" Riya said, her cheeks deepening in color.

"Because it's ancient," Haley said, dead serious, "and apparently records literally everything that's ever happened."

She tossed her hair like she'd been reading grimoires since preschool.

"Oh, and it mentioned our gloaming. You know, the whole 'you'll be immortal too once your powers kick in' thing?"

46

Riya slumped like a balloon that'd lost the will to party.

"So the powers thing is actually real," she muttered. "Great."

She stared at nothing. "I always wondered why we never fit in."

A beat.

"Now I know why. It's because we're apparently immortal weirdos in training."

"Aw, look at you," Haley said with a grin. "Catching that witchy sense."

"No, I'm not!" Riya hissed—then instantly dropped her voice. "I just... It's a lot, okay? Finding out we're basically magical misfits with a side of immortality?"

"I know," Haley said softly, reaching over to squeeze her hand. "But hey, at least now we can understand why we've always felt... off."

"Yeah," Riya muttered. "Finally, scientific proof we're weird."

She looked down at the book, heart still thumping. The whole thing felt unsettling like a fairytale left out in the rain. And their parents were icing on a five-tier cake made of secrets.

"And this book?" Riya said, eyeing it like it might blink again. "Yeah... It's definitely not just paper and ink."

Whatever it was, it had layers—deep, ancient, spine-tingling layers that felt like they were staring back.

Haley tilted her head, like she was trying to catch a whisper from the moon.

"Have you ever heard of the Rede before tonight?" she asked.

Riya snorted. "Nope. But they sound like the ancient council version of *Judgment Squad*. Like, 'we'll-curse-your-bloodline' level petty."

She paused, then added with a shiver, "Actually, scratch that. I definitely don't want a surprise run-in with Ms. Treewith anytime soon."

"Same," Haley said, giggling. "But let's be real... our moms could totally take her down."

Before Riya could agree, Haley's phone buzzed to life—screen lighting up like a flickering candle in a séance.

1:11 a.m.

"Crap," she whispered. "My mom's gonna freak. Your mom's gonna freak. You need to go home."

"But I'm freaked out," Riya said, wrapping her arms around herself. "I don't wanna be alone tonight."

"Yeah, same." Haley nodded, already tiptoeing toward the attic ladder. "Okay, I'll ask my parents if you can sleep over."

She glanced back. "But first, we've gotta hide the book. Like, seriously hide it."

47

They carefully tucked *The Book of Fates* into the caramel-colored trunk, beneath layers of old sweatshirts and half-forgotten photo albums.

Then they crept down the ladder and padded through the hallway like cats on a mission—silent, twitchy, and completely suspicious.

Haley gently nudged Raven.

One eye opened.

"Hey, Mom? Can Riya stay the night?" Haley whispered sweetly.

Raven blinked, groaned, and turned on the lamp, nudging Xavier awake. "It's so late. I thought she left hours ago."

"Nope, still here, Auntie Raven," Riya whispered, brushing hair behind her ear.

Raven sighed and texted Celeste while the cousins stood frozen like statues.

"She said okay," her mom mumbled. "Surprisingly."

The cousins mouthed a silent *yessss* and ran back to Haley's room, diving under the covers.

They twisted into their classic blanket burrito—side sleeping, pillows tucked under hips like always.

The moment their silk bonnet heads touched the pillows, sleep claimed them—drawing them into dreams of enchanted balls, hidden powers, and pages that glowed with answers.

But outside, something had slipped through the Veil.

Silent. Patient. Watching.

A creeping shadow neither of them saw.

And by morning... Nothing would be the same.

CHAPTER TEN

Two Days Before Halloween

Riya's phone alarm chimed at six-thirty in the morning, which only felt like ten minutes after she had fallen asleep.

Her bleary eyes fought to focus, unraveling like a tangled string. Then she spotted something at her feet—and jolted upright, cat-fast, heart hammering.

"U-um... Ha—ley," Riya sputtered, swiping off her alarm with a shaky hand. "Wake up... you *really* need to see this."

Haley groaned and rolled over, voice still sticky with sleep. "Ouch, ouch—ouch-hhh. What is it, Ray?"

Riya didn't answer. She just pointed to the edge of the bed. Haley blinked once... then gasped, sharp as a balloon popping inches from her face.

The Book of Fates.

Just sitting there. Calm. Innocent. Like a baby lamb that absolutely shouldn't be in Haley's room.

Her voice pitched up like a startled goat. "Okay—WHY is that book here?! Did you move it from the attic?"

"No!" Riya yelped.

Haley caught the wild fear spinning in Riya's brown eyes—like ribbons trapped in a fan—and tried to steady the air between them.

"...Maybe it's trying to tell us something," she said carefully, words balancing on a whisper, fragile as glass. "I think... I think we should stay home. Read more. Find out what it wants before it finds us again."

Riya's mouth dropped open like a tunnel entrance.

"Are you kidding me, Hales?!" she shrieked. "You're not freaked out that it followed us to your bedroom—without legs?! Or worse—what if your mom dropped it off before heading to work and now we're grounded for eternity?!"

A sudden click and clang opened the latch to Haley's door, and Raven strolled in as if walking on air.

Riya threw the covers over the book, blocking it from sight.

"Hey, girls," said Raven, "I thought I heard screaming or something. Are you two okay?"

Riya had a blank stare.

She wanted to blurt everything, but curiosity still weighed heavier than confession. Her chocolate-brown eyes flicked up, wide and restless.

"Auntie Raven," she whispered, legs prickling like pincushions. "Did you... move something after we went to bed?"

Raven jingled whatever was in her pocket—it clattered like pearls down cement stairs.

"No," she said. "I was in bed all night. Why? Missing something?"

Riya froze, positive they were caught. But then the book rustled under the blankets, like a hamster tunneling through a hoodie.

She scrambled to flatten the sheets, smothering the sound.

Haley jumped in fast, her voice too bright.

"Nope! Nothing's missing. We're fine," she rushed out. "Just... think we're getting sick or something. Late-night study session finally hit us."

Her tone was too dry, too forced. She coughed into her hand for effect, then elbowed Riya.

"Yeah, super sick," Riya muttered, coughing on cue. "Definitely no school today, Auntie."

Raven narrowed her mismatched eyes, reading them like a puzzle.

"Well... it was cold in the house last night," she said. "Any tests or homework you're behind on?"

"Nope. All caught up. No tests for a week," Haley answered—too quickly.

"...Okay," Raven said slowly, not buying it. "I'll text your mom, Riya, let her know you're staying here. Celeste and I can take the day off from to—"

"No!" Haley blurted, then tried to reel it back. "I mean... You don't have to. We can take care of ourselves. We just need some rest."

Raven raised an eyebrow.

Haley added, stumbling, "We've gotta be better by Halloween. And we're old enough to handle one sick day."

Raven gave them a long, skeptical look. The cousins did look pale. And exhausted.

Finally, she sighed.

"All right. But if you need me or Auntie Celeste, text. We'll be here faster than a broom can fly—"

She caught herself, laughed awkwardly.

"I mean... We'll drive. Obviously."

The cousins were too stunned to process the broom comment—way too on-the-nose for comfort.

The door shut with a soft *thwomp*.

Haley waited until Raven's footsteps faded and the front lock clicked.

She exhaled. "Too close." Then she grinned. "Ray, I've got a plan— Operation: *Hide the Book From Our Moms.*"

Riya shot her a look sharp enough to cut glass. "Nope. No operations, no schemes, no lies. We tell them. Now. And then we figure out how to launch this cursed thing into another dimension."

Her jaw clenched, teeth grinding against her cheek. Her brain felt like a browser with forty-seven tabs open—and none of them would stop buffering.

Haley touched her arm. "What if we just... give it a nickname? Like, Inky? Then we can talk about it without anyone catching on."

Riya blinked at her. "You want to *name* it? What's next—feeding it snacks?"

Haley shrugged. "It already writes to us. Might as well call it something."

"No," Riya said flatly. "If we name it, we're basically inviting it to stay."

The book flung the sheets back and snapped open—sudden, eager, almost playful, like a dolphin begging for a fish.

I agree—Inky suits me—many thanks.

Now... you must turn your minds to what matters.

Your parents met at the Charmwic Ball—and that night, your mothers wrought a deed that could not be undone.

A working of such powers, it bent the course of majick itself.

And from that hour forth, the cursed consequences have hunted you— shadowing every step, waiting for the day they might claim you as their own.

CHAPTER ELEVEN

Two Days Before Halloween

FROM: INKY
TO: RIYA & HALEY

It had taken your mothers the entire day to prepare for the Charmwic Ball.

Among the majick folk, entry was not granted with an invitation.

They had to earn it—with a spell so impressive, so unforgettable, it bent the air around them.

Celeste had spent hours perfecting a charm to unveil a person's deepest destiny—one even they might not yet understand. Raven, ever the tactician, crafted a Peek of Fate to glimpse how that destiny might unfold...

By sundown, their voices were hoarse from chanting, their fingertips numb from channeling.

They were lightheaded, spell-worn, and barely standing. But they were ready. Almost.

The final step: the Veil Oath. They chanted...

Tonight, the stars align
Our paths in light entwine.
We cross the silver sea.
Where all majick folk run free.
By heart and breath, so it shall be.
When they opened their eyes, the air shimmered.

Their room was gone.

Towering white pillars rose like ancient guardians. Ahead, the double doors of the Charmwic Ball stood gleaming—etched with runes, pulsing with energy.

But before your mothers could step inside, three figures blocked their path.

The Rede.

Ms. Treewith—the sternest of the three—stood front and center, robe crackling with static as if even fabric could not stand her. She raised one bony hand and sniffed.

"This year is different," she said coldly. "Expectations are higher. Your little party spells won't cut it."

Celeste straightened her spine. "According to Section 4.3 of the Charmwic Charter, all spell performance changes must be announced one month in advance."

Ms. Treewith rolled her eyes. "We will be amplifying all powers threefold tonight. We need proof you can handle it."

Raven raked her fingers through her loose waves, already bristling with annoyance. But Ms. Treewith had the Seventh Sense—she could hear wicked thoughts.

"New spell. Big spell," Raven hissed under her breath. "Did you see that Light Warrior just turn a comet into the chandelier?"

Celeste groaned. "We're sixteen in ash years. Our flashiest spell is a ten-second hair-and-makeup glam-up."

Raven gloated with a confidence Celeste had never seen before.

"I have an idea that'll blow the brooms right out of this place."

But even as she said it, her eyes lit with dangerous possibility.

Her voice dropped to a whisper. "...What if we try the Vespergate?"

Celeste's breath hitched. "No way. That incantation doesn't just open a door—it rips one right into Dahmorte."

Raven's voice dropped to a hush. "Not if we alter it. Just enough. Shift the intention... reroute the tether. We open a door—but to Coelum instead."

"That's still insanely dangerous. The Vespergate is Shadow Veil majick. If you're not... then..."

"We've got Waykit in our blood. Which means any spell or power our family's ever touched, like, a bajillion years—we can try. Dad used it. Maybe we can, too."

"Or maybe it'll kill us."

Raven shrugged. "Only one way to find out."

Together, they stepped forward.

Celeste's fingers traced ancient spirals in the air. Raven drew power from the shadows, her astral magic flaring like starlight under pressure.

56

Crack!

Their palms met.

BOOM.

The ballroom vanished—replaced by a dreamscape spun from clouds and wonder.

The grass exhaled. Light rippled across the field. Around them, hearts softened like paper lanterns set free into the sky.

And overhead... the moon shifted. Its silver glow deepened, bleeding into a rich, violet haze.

Even Ms. Haute raised an eyebrow. Yet Ms. Treewith? Still unimpressed—but the octopus-colored doors groaned open anyway.

Raven and Celeste stepped inside. The majick hit them like honey melting into hot tea.

Tiny besoms—ostrich-feather brooms—zipped overhead, dodging outstretched hands. Catch one, and you earn a wish.

Silvermoths—gigantic, head-sized moths—no longer feared, drifted through the dancers, their wings scattering light as they delivered parchment love notes that shimmered like stardust.

A Mooshi—a plump, glowing energy mouse—kissed a Tiant, one of the mountain-moving beasts.

Celeste's eyes swept the room, widening at the feast. Above the buffet, plates hovered politely, drifting in neat rows as if waiting their turn to be chosen.

Raven beelined for dessert. Celeste took a cautious bite of everything. But something uneasy crackled beneath the glamour.

Raven glanced sideways, voice low. "If I used Shadow forces for the Vespergate... could that pass to our kids?"

Celeste went still. "Rae—the Vespergate changed the moon. That wasn't a side effect. That was a warning."

Raven swallowed hard. "Think we'll get in trouble with the Rede?"

Celeste shook her head. "Forget the Rede. You had shadows tailing you. Your eyes went lavender. Like *hers*."

Raven paled. "No way."

"Way. And now the moon looks like it's bleeding grape soda."

Celeste narrowed her eyes. "Remember, this disaster was *your* idea."

Raven's voice threaded softly through the majick.

"Well, it'sa good thing a sister's bond is stronger than anything."

Celeste's gaze lingered on the glowing archway. "Even if we don't come back the same?"

Raven's answer came as a whisper, steady and unshaken.

"Especially then."

But it was already too late. The Vespergate had begun to change them.

Raven would soon bear a scar at the back of her neck—jagged, the size of an apple slice. Her eyes, mismatched. One of them—no longer hers.

Celeste's hair would frost white at the tips, a spell-streaked warning she could never shake.

The consequences had not arrived yet. But they were coming.

CHAPTER TWELVE

Two Days Before Halloween

Life as Riya and Haley knew it had officially flipped upside down.

Their moms? Secretly powerful sorceresses.

Their dads? Still a mystery—but definitely not ordinary.

Everything felt like it had been yanked right out of a twisted fairy tale and dropped in their laps—no warning, no user manual.

But what shocked Riya the most wasn't the spellcasting or the life-risking rituals. It was the creatures.

They were so bizarre, so entirely not of this world, they made reality feel like a fever dream on overdrive.

"Okay, can I just say—holy H!" Riya gasped, tugging at the hem of her sleep shirt like it owed her answers.

"Those Mooshis and Tiants? Creepy, but also weirdly adorable. And our moms doing the Ves-per-g-gate," she was still getting used to the words, "even though it could've killed them? Are you freaking kidding me?!"

Haley didn't answer.

Riya kept going like a busted fire hydrant, all pressure and no pause.

"We might have powers, Hales. Like... actual powers. Good and bad." She hesitated, fumbling for the word. "Because of... uh, Waykit, or whatever it's called."

Riya shook her head. "Our moms were like walking spell-slinging legends. I can't even picture us doing that."

Haley finally spoke, her voice small.

"Yeah. Waykit," Haley muttered, staring at the floor like it might explain something.

"Why would my mom even do that? Knowing she could pass down bad stuff. Like... Maldrop. I think that's what Inky called it—evil."

She swallowed hard.

"Why would she risk it?"

"Maybe she didn't think she'd have kids," Riya said gently. "So it didn't feel like a big deal."

"I don't know," Haley murmured.

"I get it. I'm scared too," Riya said, her voice softening. "But if there's even a chance we inherited something messed up from our parents..." She looked at Haley. "Don't you want to know what that is?"

Haley tugged at her curls, sliding to the edge of the bed. "Great. Now you're the curious one, and I'm the freaked-out mess. We totally switched roles."

Riya let out a crooked smile. "Yeah, well... surprises suck. And not knowing what's coming? Even worse. I'd rather be ready."

For her, information meant power. Knowing their family history—no matter how chaotic—felt like the only thing keeping her grounded.

For Haley, a small part of her liked knowing she was different. But what if her powers were twisted? What if she tried to turn a piece of paper into a notebook and accidentally summoned a toad that breathed fire?

"We're supposed to do that gloaming thing to unlock our powers. But what if someone at school finds out we're... magical?" She swallowed. "Audrey and Sarah would annihilate us."

Riya pulled the blanket up to her nose, her stomach twisting in knots. All she wanted was a normal life. But after everything they'd read... she knew that ship had sailed, sunk, even.

Haley slid closer, her voice barely above a whisper.

"I don't know if knowing more will make things better. But..." —she paused, eyes shadowed with doubt— "I think I might be evil."

A rustle sounded at the foot of the bed.

Then—CLAP.

Inky slammed shut with a dramatic *thud*.

"Ooh, we made Inky mad," Haley teased.

"Whatever! It acts like we're supposed to be experts already," Riya huffed. "Creepy shadow parties, spells blowing up in people's faces—it's a lot. We need a break."

Riya and Haley trudged downstairs. The middle stair let out its usual dramatic squeak.

"Ugh, will someone please fix that cursed step already?" Riya groaned.

The house stayed silent. The clock on the oven blinked **12:30 pm.**

"No wonder I'm starving," Riya muttered, yanking open the fridge.

But everything looked... off.

Leftovers she usually loved suddenly seemed weird and slimy. The thought of inheriting a bag of damaged spells and hand-me-down hexes made her stomach lurch.

Haley rustled through the pantry and pulled out a cereal box. Riya followed, grabbing nut milk, two bowls, and mismatched spoons. They ate at the counter, side by side.

"This kinda feels like something our moms used to do," Riya said between bites. "You think we'll always be this close?"

"Duh. My mom says a sister's love is stronger than anything. And since we're cousins..." Haley grinned. "That's basically double the love."

They laughed, spooning cereal into their mouths—until a sharp thump echoed from upstairs like a rabbit snapping its foot.

A scuffle followed, heavy and uneven, as if something was being dragged across the floor.

The cousins froze. Another thud. And then—CRASH.

Spitting sparks that hissed, as if eager to torch the house, Inky hurled itself down the stairs and hit the last step with a slap of parchment and a puff of dust—mad as ever, skittering forward on its corners like a deranged crab.

"UM—RAY!" Haley shrieked, scrambling to her feet.

Riya's face drained to seafoam green. "Inky is demented!"

The book flapped toward them like a rabid goose on a mission.

Riya screamed and lunged for a kitchen knife.

"BACK OFF!" she shouted, brandishing it like she actually knew what she was doing.

"Ray, seriously? You'll probably end up paper-cutting a spell and dooming us both!" Haley shouted, swatting at her. "Put that down!"

"Too late! I'm carving that thing like a Thanksgiving turkey!"

Inky jumped like a panther and crash-landed on the counter, cereal flying like confetti.

Its pages flurried until a new page slammed open.

I'm not trying to scare you...
BUT MAYBE I SHOULD!
There is no time to run from your Fates.
Everyone depends on it!

Riya—older by two whole minutes—slammed her palms onto the counter, making a jar of peanut butter wobble dangerously.

"Look, Inky—we need a break. And you need to be okay with that!"

Inky fluttered its pages like a furious bird in a cage, parchment snapping with rage.

Then—

Ding-dong.

The doorbell rang. Sharp. Sudden. Too loud.

The cousins went still. Like prey.

Riya's breath caught. Haley's eyes darted to the window.

No one moved. The book went silent.

Even the refrigerator hum seemed to fade.

Then—

Ding-dong.

Again.

Longer this time.

Like someone was waiting.

CHAPTER THIRTEEN

TWO DAYS BEFORE HALLOWEEN

"Please don't be the neighbors," Riya whispered, barely breathing.

Riya crept to the door as if it might bite.

The floorboard beneath her foot let out a soft groan.

She gripped the handle, hesitated—then cracked it open an inch.

Two familiar faces stared back.

"Audrey? Sarah?" Riya blinked. "What are you doing here?"

Audrey smirked, her voice syrupy and slow.

"Our moms let us skip school," she said with a shrug.

"Yeah," Sarah added, her voice high and eager. "We can basically do whatever we want. So... we figured we'd help with decorations!"

"That's... nice," Riya said, forcing a smile. "We were up late picking costumes, so our moms let us sleep in."

"Cool, cool," Audrey said, stepping forward. "You gonna let us in?"

"Yeah!" Sarah beamed. "We'll make your party chaos, but, like, the fun kind."

Riya froze.

Inky was still flapping faintly on the kitchen counter like it sensed something.

"Uh... we're kinda tired, and things are a little weird right now," she said carefully. "Maybe later?"

Haley shot her a look, then stepped just far enough from the doorway so Audrey and Sarah couldn't hear.

"Why are you pushing them away?" she whispered, brows furrowed.

Riya leaned in, voice low. "Ynki... Yaleh."

Their secret code. *Inky... Haley.* Words reversed.

Haley's eyes widened. She immediately nodded.

"Yeah, we're super tired," Haley said quickly. "Rain check?"

Audrey tilted her head, her smile too sweet to be real. "Come on—just say the words. Invite us in."

Riya's eyes narrowed. "Why do you keep saying that? You've never talked like that before."

Sarah rolled her eyes. "It's how classy people talk, duh. So are you letting us in or not?"

A chill threaded through Riya's chest. Something was wrong.

"No," she said firmly. "We'll see you at our party."

Audrey and Sarah turned sharply—unnaturally in sync, like twin stick bugs on the same branch.

No goodbye. No glance back.

Just a synchronized strut down the walkway, stiff and silent, like puppets on invisible strings.

Riya and Haley didn't speak. Even Inky had gone still, its pages clamped shut like it was holding its breath.

The silence pressed in, heavy, wrong.

Haley shifted nervously. "Riya... you totally made them mad."

Riya shot her a look. "Oh, please. You wanted them walking in on a flying book and cereal carnage all over the floor?"

Haley groaned and dropped into a chair at the island, limbs flopping like she was done with everything.

"Don't even start," Riya said. "You know I'm right."

"Yeah, yeah," Haley mumbled, dragging a hand over her face. "I just don't know if we can actually pull this party off without help."

Riya blinked at her. "Seriously? You're still thinking about the party?"

Behind them, Inky rustled, its pages shivering before fresh words began to curl across the paper.

Who was that at the door?

"No one!" Haley snapped. "Just people, Riya didn't want to see your dramatic entrance."

Inky flipped to another page.

Good.
Do not let anyone in.

From now on, everyone is a threat.
Focus. No phones. No distractions.
OR I'LL SHOW YOU WHAT'S AT STAKE.

Riya groaned. "We've already met a self-writing, breathing, future-predicting book with an attitude. What else could possibly freak us out?"

Naturally, Inky took that as a challenge.

Its pages gave a smug little flutter, as if it were already plotting how to make Riya wish she were either a full-blown witch... or dead.

CHAPTER FOURTEEN

Two Days Before Halloween

Pots clanged. Cereal boxes exploded. Inky's pages thrashed like wings. The air reeked of scorched metal, a chill snapped across the cousins' skin. Then—

A storm of lightning and smoke swallowed the kitchen, vanishing the instant a screaming tunnel tore itself into existence.

It howled like wind through dense trees, its walls writhing with streaks of light and shadow that twisted into impossible patterns, like the hides of wild beasts.

Air ripped past—cold, savage, unending—like the void was shrink-wrapping them for oblivion.

SPLASH.

They hit something slick and warm. The kitchen was gone.

In its place sprawled a gooey, humid cavern that stank of lost hopes, broken dreams, and moldy socks.

Slime wept down the curved walls. Overhead, a thin, skin-like film stretched taut, glowing the sickly shade of clotted blood. The floor throbbed beneath them—soft, fleshy, alive.

Riya's scream caught in her throat as the truth hit: this wasn't a cave. She and Haley had landed in something's belly.

Before she could utter another word, the monster sucked them deeper. *SLURP.*

"NOT OKAY!" Riya shrieked as the world tilted and they were slurped down like living spaghetti.

71

They shot through slick tunnels that squeezed and churned, every twist groaning like a stomach trying to digest them. Slime clung to their skin.

And then—

THUD.

They slammed into solid ground.

The cousins were in a hollow chamber now—dark, jagged, echoing. The air felt electric, the silence too loud.

The walls were stone, but not natural. Chiseled. Scarred. As if something had tried to claw its way out.

Gargoyle-shaped statues leered from alcoves, their eyes glowing faintly red.

Riya pushed herself up, heart hammering. "Note to self: Inky doesn't do dares. It does nightmares."

She swallowed hard. "Do you think it's done with us?"

Haley's hand trembled as she pointed to a faint glow in the far corner.

"Look..." Her voice was low, uneven. "There's your answer."

A ghost drifted forward from the shadows—slow, deliberate, like it had all the time in the world and none to spare.

Its eyes were sunken voids, twin abysses where light went to die. Its mouth was stitched shut with thread dark as ink, knotted tight, like it carried secrets it wasn't allowed to speak.

Riya's cry tore from her throat. She scrambled back, heart pounding, and snatched up the nearest thing—a cracked, moss-covered skull—clutching it like a shield.

The ghost didn't flinch.

Instead, it lifted a translucent arm and unrolled a glowing scroll from the folds of its tattered robes.

The parchment shimmered with ancient light, its surface etched in fine golden ink—the same ink Inky used to write itself.

Riya blinked. It was a family tree—*their* family tree.

Names curled and spiraled across the scroll, each one glowing like fireflies in the dark—Ama, Henry, Manchester, Xavier, Raven, Celeste...

But at the bottom, Riya's breath hitched.

Two blank boxes. Empty. Waiting.

"Why are ours blank?" she whispered, still gripping the skull.

Haley's voice shook, barely louder than the ghost's breath. "Because if we fail... we might never exist."

The scroll dissolved into ash.

Then—

A wet, inhuman growl cut the dark. Then the shadows unpeeled, and something oozed out, dripping decay.

The Gloze had arrived.

CHAPTER FIFTEEN

Two Days Before Halloween

The stench hit first—rotting meat and wet earth.

So strong it punched the air out of Haley's lungs and made Riya gag.

Then a snarl—a wet, guttural sound that vibrated through the chamber walls like a death rattle.

A forked tongue flicked between jagged teeth, hissing like steam from a cracked pipe.

Haley yanked Riya back just as the shadows split open. A hulking shape pushed through—dripping, snarling, eyes burning like extinguished coals.

The Gloze's body was a grotesque puzzle—limbs too long, bending where nothing should, bones pressing against sagging skin, stitched from wounds that never healed and things that refused to stay buried.

Its hands—if you could call them that—ended in twisted beaks, clacking open and shut as it grasped at the air.

Riya and Haley screamed in perfect harmony.

Above them, Inky swooped down, spitting words like shrapnel—a storm of black letters that circled them like furious crows.

DO NOT RUN.
DO NOT SCREAM.
DO NOT MAKE EYE CONTACT.
OR YOUR UNO WILL BE LOST FOREVER!

"I think we already broke all three rules!" Riya screamed.

Words flashed again, scorched into the smoky air by Inky's unforgiving ink.

This is Dahmorte's Gloze.
Foreboding. Malefic. A hunger for fresh onus in its every breath.
Fail... and it shall devour you. All whom you love will perish.
The Fates will fall—and the fault will be yours alone.

The Gloze stepped closer, grinning like it had just unwrapped fresh gifts on its eternal, cursed birthday. Its breath rolled out in a fetid wave—scorched paper and spoiled milk.

"OKAY, WE GET IT!" Riya shouted, hands over her eyes. "Message received! Loud and traumatizing!"

And just like that—*WHOOSH.*

A flash of blinding light. A jolt like static hit the cousins' heads. The ground vanished beneath them.

They blinked—and were back in the kitchen.

Cereal littered the floor like a sugar-coated crime scene.

Milk dripped slowly down the cabinet doors, one sticky glob at a time.

The room smelled like toasted sugar and burnt marshmallow... somehow.

Haley wobbled on her feet. Riya was still clutching Haley's arm like a seatbelt.

"Okay. Note to self," she whispered, still trembling. "Don't ever—like ever—dare Inky again."

Haley didn't laugh.

She stared at the book like it might launch another horror show any second.

It was a bad sign that Inky could apparently teleport them right into what looked—and smelled—like actual hell.

Now there was no choice. Disobey, and it wouldn't just yell or dump them in a slime tunnel—it might hand the keys of a cursed world to some slobbering, snake-tongued monster.

Inky lay calmly on the kitchen counter, pages fluttering like it hadn't just staged a full-on interdimensional nightmare.

It flipped itself open, perfectly serene.

Good.
Now, where was I?
Ah, yes—your mothers—and the Vespergate...

CHAPTER SIXTEEN

Two Days Before Halloween

FROM: INKY
TO: RIYA & HALEY

It began... when Celeste and Raven performed the Vespergate and believed they had escaped the cost.

They were grievously mistaken.

Then—came the cloaks. The Rede swept in like thunderclouds across the ballroom.

It wasn't just their speed—it was the look in Ms. Treewith's eyes.

"YOU TWO—NOW!" she barked, her voice a mix of fear and fury.

Celeste and Raven followed the Rede without argument. The silver double doors opened—then slammed shut with a BOOM.

Inside, gold vines curled along the stone walls. A chipped gargoyle glared at them from beneath a wilted flowerpot. It guarded a teal-blue door that looked like it belonged in a haunted maze.

Ms. Treewith kicked him aside. "Out of the way, slowpoke."

Celeste and Raven exchanged a quick, *sorry* glance at the statue, then followed the cloaked figures down a strange corridor.

The walls pulsed with breathing spikes. The floor curled like a taco shell, forcing them into a single-file line.

Empty picture frames lined the walls—hundreds of them. Some tilted. Some cracked. All pulsing with a strange, silvery shimmer that made the air feel too thin.

Raven made the mistake of looking into one of them. A face screamed back.Not hers. Rotting. Hollow-eyed. Skin peeling like wet paper.

She stumbled back, hand flying to her face. "Don't—don't look at the walls!" she gasped.

Too late.

Celeste's gaze had already locked with one of the frames. It was her reflection—but twisted. Bruised. Decomposed. Her cheeks sunken, lips blackened, eyes clouded over like glass marbles.

She jerked free, breath ragged. Her voice cracked to a whisper. "Where are they taking us?!"

Raven didn't answer—they were practically sprinting now.

The corridor stretched endlessly ahead, swallowing every sound. Behind them, the picture frames began to rattle.

Seven doors in, Ms. Haute glanced back. "Hurry! We don't have much time!"

Then—

They stopped in front of a monstrous black door in a rotten apple-shaped room.

It sagged with skulls molded into its surface, as if pressed there by desperate hands. Their sockets stared back—hollow, yet weighted with verdicts that never stopped murmuring.

Celeste's jaw unhinged. "That's—the Door of Bones? Tell me you're not seriously considering tossing us in there?"

Ms. Treewith didn't speak. She just nodded once.

"But the Vespergate wasn't a crime!" Celeste protested. "We brought love to the ball. That has to count for something!"

"You drew from two opposing Veils," Ms. Treewith snapped. "That tipped the Fates toward Shadow. And the Vespergate," her eyes narrowed— "that was your key into the ball. A key taken for personal gain."

"Everyone used spells tonight to get in!"

"They brought real offerings. You didn't."

"Love is real!" Celeste shouted.

"Not according to the Hive," Ms. Treewith said, her voice cold and certain.

She paused, taking a deliberate step forward—just enough for Celeste and Raven to catch the sharp bounce of her tight, frizzed curls, springing around her gaunt face like coiled wire with a mind of their own.

"The Hive does not care about comfort," Ms. Treewith said coolly. "Only truth. Only what hides in your Shadow—your Fates."

She frowned. "You pass—or you perish."

Raven's fists clenched.

"This is so messed up. We should be celebrated for what we did—not punished."

80

Ms. Treewith's expression didn't flicker. Her voice cut the air like ice.

"Child, the Fates do not celebrate—they tally."

The exit behind them slammed shut with a thunderous *boom*. The sound echoed like a final verdict.

They were trapped.

Then the Door of Bones creaked open, oozing a smell like burnt hair and rotten citrus.

Celeste burst into tears. "WAIT! Please, have mercy! We're not ready!"

Mr. Seacoal raised his scepter. "No more stalling. Face your Fates."

The door yawned wider. Mist curled like smoke around their ankles.

With one final lasso, Celeste and Raven fell forward—into the black. Swallowed whole.

CHAPTER SEVENTEEN

TWO DAYS BEFORE HALLOWEEN

Haley sat frozen. The echo of her mom being tossed inside still clawed at her ribs—swallowed by the Door of Bones like it was alive. Hungry.

Riya's lips were pressed thin, and her eyes were already hard with resolve.

She'd seen this coming—the ending to their moms' story. She was always ahead, already smelling the coffee before it was done brewing.

Haley, meanwhile, felt like she was always behind. Late to the terror. Late to the truth. Late to everything. Even born two minutes after Riya... Late.

And in that quiet, ugly moment, she knew the truth: she wasn't ready. Not even close.

She shoved the thought down, masking it with false confidence. Pretending she wasn't already slipping behind.

Haley blinked hard. "The Door of Bones? Inky's kidding, right? It sounds like nightmare fuel."

Riya gave a slow, grim nod. "Because it is."

"How did we not know any of this before?" Haley muttered, tugging at her sagging blue sleep socks. They bunched awkwardly at her ankles, like even they were overwhelmed.

Riya leaned against the kitchen island, drumming her fingers on the edge.

"Probably because our moms screwed up that spell. And they didn't want us finding out."

Haley looked up, frowning. "Screwed up how?"

"They didn't exactly think it through before casting it," Riya said. Her voice was calm. Too calm—like she'd already played every version of this truth in her head. "The Door of Bones is brutal. But maybe... it's the wake-up call we needed."

Her eyes flicked to Haley's.

"If we screw this up, it's over. For them. For us. For everything."

She let out a hard breath.

"So we need to get our act together. Like... now, now."

It hadn't taken her long to piece it together. When their moms were their age, they were already casting massive spells—the kind that ripped open dimensions.

Celeste had somehow come back with one foot still in the Light.

But Raven? She hadn't come back the same. She came back twisted. Changed.

There was no room for mistakes now.

Riya and Haley had to master their powers—yesterday because the next wrong move wouldn't just cost them the fight. It could cost them everything.

The thought slammed into Riya like a stone. She ran her fingers along the countertop, as if playing an invisible piano.

"Take it from me," Riya said coolly, propping her elbow on the counter. "Majick is dangerous."

"You sound like your mom," Haley teased, half smiling.

"I'm serious, Hales! Doesn't it freak you out that if we mess up—like our moms—it could be the end? Like, actual end-of-the-world type stuff!" Riya cried, shaking out her caramel-colored hands.

"Yeah, I guess," Haley muttered. "But I already feel like we're flunking magic school—if that's even a thing."

"It *is* a thing," Riya snapped. "Aetherion Academy. It's where we do our gloaming and get our powers. Were you even listening to Inky?"

Haley frowned, shoulders curling inward.

She *had* been listening... sort of. But ever since learning about Waykit, her thoughts kept looping like a broken music stream—stuck on the same scary song.

She felt like a ticking time bomb, T-minus meltdown—either learn to harness her shadow energy, or get swallowed by it.

And deep down, she knew the only way to survive was to keep digging—into Inky, into the past, into the truth.

"I *have* been listening," Haley grumbled. "And the Door of Bones sounds seriously messed up. Like, why would the Rede make our moms do that?"

"I think Inky mentioned it once—something about personal gain," Riya said, brushing a curl from her face. "Still feels like major punishment overkill."

84

"Exactly! Something about the Rede doesn't sit right with me," Haley muttered. "Feels like they care more about control than people."

Riya shivered. "It's not even the power that scares me. It's all the rules we don't know."

"Rules." Haley let out a soft laugh, then sighed. "You've always been good at following them. Maybe I should start, too... before it's, you know, too late."

A flash of terror flickered across Haley's face—so fast it might've been missed, if not for how still she went afterward.

She stared off, silent, eyes wide as a low creak echoed from somewhere deep in the house.

Wood settling... or something else?

Her mouth opened like she was about to speak—but Riya had already grabbed Inky and bolted, her footsteps thundering up the stairs.

"Hey! Ray, wait up!" Haley called, chasing after her.

Racing up the steps, Haley almost forgot they'd just learned they might fail and face a soul-eating door right out of a nightmare. For a heartbeat, it felt like a game of chase. She giggled after Riya—until—

Halfway up, her foot snagged.

Squeak.

She froze.

A faint shimmer pulsed beneath the middle step—thin, flickering, like a reflection that didn't belong.

Haley squinted, heart hammering. *Had Inky knocked something loose on its way down?*

"Um, Ray?" Her voice wavered now. "You might want to come back down here..."

Riya stopped at the top of the stairs, turning slowly. Something in Haley's voice—tight, careful—made the hair on her arms rise.

Then it happened.

The step pulsed. Once. Twice.

With a soft hiss, the wood cracked open like an eyelid snapping awake.

A sliver of darkness spilled out—thick and slow, like oil sliding on top of water.

And from somewhere below... something breathed.

Not air. Not wind. A presence.

And it wasn't just watching.

It was waiting. And it knew their names.

CHAPTER EIGHTEEN

Two Days Before Halloween

Riya huffed beside Haley, Inky tucked under one arm like a football. "What now?" she hissed, "If this is another one of Inky's pranks, I swear I'll—"

She stopped mid-sentence. Froze.

Haley was pointing. Her finger didn't tremble, but her voice did.

"What is that?" she whispered.

A faint glow shimmered beneath the middle step. Not bright—just pulsing, like the heartbeat of a moonbeam.

The air around it felt colder, heavier, like it had been exhaled from a different world.

"No clue," Riya murmured. "But let's pretend we didn't see it and go upstairs like smart people."

Haley raised a brow. "Yeah, no. We're checking it out."

She crouched and pressed her fingers to the wood. It felt oddly soft, like it didn't want to be part of the staircase anymore. With a slow peel—like removing an old sticker—Haley pulled the board back.

A gap yawned beneath it—not a crack, not a crawlspace. But something new. Spiraling into thick, black air.

It didn't creak. It breathed. The darkness tugged at the drifting dust, pulling it inward—greedy... alive.

Riya blinked, wide-eyed. "Okay. Ew. Creepy basement. Nope."

She leaned against the railing, trying to catch her breath—and accidentally nudged something.

Click. A lever.

The stairs groaned, then shifted like an old trapdoor and creaked open.

Beneath them, a stone staircase spiraled into darkness—just wide enough for Riya and Haley to slip through. But neither moved.

One by one, each step lit up with a sickly green glow, rimmed in flickering neon like something half-alive, half-hexed.

A rush of cold air burst up from the void. It smelled like damp stone... and something else. Older. Wilder.

Riya's mind screamed *no.* The last thing she needed was to be blindsided by more family secrets—one more childhood trauma waiting to haunt her into adulthood.

"I think you already know what I'm thinking," she said, voice shaky, "but I'll say it anyway—we should *not* go down there."

Haley's eyes glittered with wonder—a secret room. Maybe more spells, treasures... truths.

"Then you know what I'll say," she smirked, already taking the first step.

"Wait—Hales!" Riya darted into the kitchen. She came back with a tiny flashlight, its beam slicing through the dark and skimming over jagged stone steps.

"Ew," she muttered. Then, with a wince, "Okay... here we go."

They linked arms and took the first two steps, inching forward like terrified geckos creeping toward the edge of a limb.

Haley leaned in. "Did you hear that?"

From below, something whispered the word—

Finally.

Riya's heart nearly exploded.

She clutched Haley's arm tighter. "Did that voice just say... something?!"

She spun around, ready to bolt—But the trapdoor slammed shut above them. They fell. A brutal drop, like the floor had given up on holding them.

Thud.

They landed in a tangled heap on cold, unforgiving stone.

"You've gotta be kidding me..." Riya muttered, brushing dust from her face. Her voice echoed strangely, as if the walls were made of memory foam instead of brick.

Mounted on the wall hung a grotesque head, pale flesh stretched too tight over bone. Hairless. Window-sized. Its glassy eyes stared forward, locked in an eternal snarl.

Six twisted tusks jutted from its jowls like broken tree limbs, and where its nose should've been was a warped, human-sized hook—bent into the shape of a question mark.

88

Haley stepped back. "That's not taxidermy."

Riya grimaced. "Nope. That's a wall-mounted proof I'll be in therapy forever."

A small silver plaque shimmered beneath the beast's chin, half-buried in cobwebs.

Riya reached out, eyes narrowing as she read aloud:
She who gazes upon this boar
Shall roam no more.
Ahead is a door of ancient lore—
Lightwices, enter, to the core.
And take what waits inside the drawer.

"Ugh, gross. A creepy little poem that rhymes?" Riya recoiled, brushing off invisible cobwebs like the words had touched her. "Hard pass." She turned toward the stairs.

A gust of wind—nowhere and everywhere—whistled through the chamber. Somewhere behind the beast's snout, something clicked.

It was enough to make Riya keep her eyes and flashlight on the ground— the only thing that hadn't betrayed her. Yet.

The walls crept in tighter with every step, the air thinning as the light began to fade. It was darker now. Colder.

The ceiling dipped. The air smelled like forgotten velvet and candle smoke.

Up ahead, a narrow blue door waited. Still. Silent. Watching.

It looked impossibly out of place. Faded, crooked, and streaked with age. Its paint peeled in long curling strips, revealing the raw wood beneath like old skin.

Haley slowed her steps. "Why does this feel like we're walking into a haunted antique store?"

Riya didn't answer. She was too busy trying not to touch anything.

Haley reached forward and grabbed the blemished brass knob, fingers hesitant.

She twisted. SCREEEEEECH.

The old metal screamed like it hadn't been touched in a hundred years.

Riya winced, one eye squinting. "Well, that didn't sound cursed at all."

Haley shot her a look. "Only one way to find out."

And with that, the door creaked open—into darkness.

Thick, velvet dark. The kind that didn't just hide things... it waited.

Then—

Scuttle. Zip. *Thump.*

Something small and fast darted past their feet.

Haley jumped back with a yelp. "What was that?!"

Riya pointed, wide-eyed. A gray blur skidded to a stop a few feet away and blinked up at them with curious, oversized eyes.

It was no ordinary mouse.

Its head was shaped like a lightbulb, glowing faintly from within—soft amber, like a nightlight. Its ears were enormous and floppy, twitching like antennae. And its potbelly jiggled with every bounce as it hopped in place, sniffing the air.

Riya gasped, clasping her hands like she'd just seen a baby dragon. "It's a Mooshi!"

She dropped to her knees, beaming. "Aww, it's *so* cute in real life!"

The Mooshi tilted its head and emitted a soft chiming noise, like wind passing through tiny bells.

Haley frowned. "Cute? It looks like someone crossbred a hamster with a lava lamp."

Riya extended a hand slowly. "Come here, little guy..."

The Mooshi blinked again—and sneezed a spark.

It darted toward the door, but Haley blocked it. "It can't get out! This little guy's way too weird for the real world." She tried to corner it, but it glided into the shadows.

Haley slammed the door shut, which rattled the room. The faint upstairs light vanished.

"We should find that drawer and get out of here," Riya grumbled, glancing nervously over her shoulder. "Before something else with a glowing nose shows up."

Haley didn't respond. She was staring at the center of the room, eyes fixed.

Without a word, she reached up, grabbed the string on a lone dangling bulb—and pulled.

Click.

The light buzzed to life.

What it revealed across the dank basement was something the cousins had never seen before—and wished they never had.

Because from that moment on, their lives would never be the same.

One of them would become a killer. And the other would help her do it.

CHAPTER NINETEEN

Two Days Before Halloween

Rows of shelves groaned beneath the weight of impossible objects—strange artifacts, weapons from nowhere they knew, all gleaming in the dim light like secrets waiting to be claimed.

Blades that shimmered with starlight. Staffs humming softly, their crystal tips glowing in rhythm with each breath.

Glass orbs floating in midair, pulsing with swirling smoke. Daggers wrapped in ivy. Swords carved from bone. Bows strung with silver threads that twitched on their own.

Riya's stomach flipped.

"What is this place?"

Haley forced a laugh, but it cracked halfway out of her chest.

Riya's gaze snagged on something strange—a balloon-shaped object, like a tiny mouse was trapped inside.

Her fingers hovered over it—until it twitched. Tiny metal teeth lining the flap clacked together like a warning.

She yanked her hand back.

"Okay... noted."

Riya turned slowly toward Haley, her expression caught somewhere between *what even is my life* and *please let this be a prank.*

"So... did you know your parents were hoarding a bunch of magical murder weapons, or is that just, like, a fun Lightwice family secret?"

Haley shook her head, still dazed. "No... my mom sells incense and vintage jeans. The most dangerous thing she's ever done is set off the smoke detector with sage."

She let out a shaky breath, her eyes scanning the surreal scene.

"This?" she whispered. "This is new."

She stepped cautiously toward a cast-iron raven's head mounted to a slender rod. Its eyes were made of tiny black gems that shimmered faintly—even without light.

Haley froze, fingertips trembling just shy of the surface. "This... is what a real witch would carry."

Riya moved closer. "Uh, Hales? Maybe don't touch the bird stick that might curse your soul?"

The metal pulsed—once.

"DON'T!" Riya yelped.

Haley backed away, eyes wide. "I didn't mean to—"

HSSSSSS.

Too late.

The raven's head rattled, coughing out a fog that spilled fast and cold, curling across the floor in snaking tendrils.

Riya spun toward the exit—only to slam into a bare wall. The door was gone.

Her breath hitched. "It vanished when you touched that raven thing!"

Haley clawed at the stone, nails screeching against the cold surface.

The fog surged higher, snaking around their legs like icy shackles.

Behind them, the raven's head hissed again—longer this time, savoring its prize.

Then—an impossible sound, one that had no business existing in any basement, magical or not.

It started as a roar—low, guttural, too close—then unraveled midair, thinning to a crackle, like paper catching fire... and finally slithering into a serpent's hiss.

Riya clamped both hands over her mouth. *That wasn't me*, she tried to say.

But what ripped out instead was a bear's growl, deep and raw, so heavy she swore she could taste musk and damp earth on her tongue.

Riya staggered back, breath catching. "What is—"

Another roar tore loose before she could finish.

Haley went rigid, eyes wide—then her lips twitched.

The sound that burst out wasn't laughter. It pitched too high, cracked in the middle, then warped into a hyena's cackle—wild and feral.

When she tried to speak, the words dissolved into snarls and screeches, as if her throat had been taken over by something savage.

Then—silence.

The fog froze. The air went still.

The raven scepter pulsed once—then slurped the mist back into its beak with a wet, gurgling hiss, like a smoothie through a straw.

The room cleared like nothing had happened.

Riya cautiously tested her voice. "Woohoo?"

Normal.

She let out a breath. "Okay. That was... bizarre."

Haley wiped tears from her eyes, still breathless from laughing. "We could totally prank someone with that."

Riya shot her a look. "Yeah—let's just not prank *us* next time."

She turned—and froze. The door was back. Tall. Closed. Wrong. Like it had been waiting for her to notice.

Then—*click.*

"Haley?" she called, her voice small.

No answer.

Riya's chest cinched tight. She took one step forward—only one—and froze.

That was when she realized.

There was another room. And Haley had either slipped inside... or was gone forever.

CHAPTER TWENTY

Two Days Before Halloween

Riya nearly dropped Inky as she tore through the piles of weapons—daggers, staffs, blades that hummed faintly in her grip.

Then her fingers caught on a small lever bolted to the table, gleaming bright blue like seaglass sunk to the ocean floor.

Without thinking, she flicked it.

Click.

The floor lurched—then spun beneath her, like the world had just decided to redraw its own map.

A seam split open, swallowing the dust, and when it cleared, she stood at the threshold of a narrow chamber that smelled of old wool and centuries left to rot.

"Ray!" Haley's voice cut through, sharp with relief. She stood across the space, already pointing. "I think I found the drawer."

Dust filmed its surface, the brass handles gone dull and green with age, yet the whole thing looked unsettlingly normal—too normal, as if it didn't belong, or worse, was only pretending to.

Haley eased the top drawer open.

Inside lay a red velvet box and, beside it, a sleek double-edged blade no longer than a pen. It shimmered, edges impossibly clean, the glass-black handle etched with symbols neither of them recognized.

Riya reached in and picked it up.

"Ouch!" She yelped, jerking her hand back. "That's... like radioactive hot!"

Haley didn't hesitate. She lifted it with both hands—calm, steady—turning it over like a childhood toy rediscovered.

The blade didn't burn.

It didn't even glow.

Riya blinked hard. "Okay, how are you not sizzling like a grilled cheese right now?"

Haley didn't answer right away. She just kept staring at the blade like it had spoken to her in a language only she could hear.

"I don't know," she said softly. "It just... feels like it's mine."

Riya wiped the box clean and read:

Behold the Athame blade—cursed, mighty, and bound by the Fates.

With a *snap*, Inky wriggled free of Riya's grip and flapped open on the dresser. The words unfurled like an ancient ribbon.

Children of Lightwice.

Welcome to your parents' Chamber of Majick—a vault of legacy, a place of truth. A room not built, but earned. What was hidden... must now be known.

The Fika

—A heat-seeking bow, carved from the fossilized teeth of Gurnish beasts. Once used to hunt onu eaters in the Third Eclipse War. It may only be drawn with a clear purpose, or it will turn on the wielder.

The Onuks

—Twin blades infused with Fate-thread. Capable of slicing through spells, immortality, curses, and even time... at a cost.

The Aza

—Xavier Garlock's three-barrelled pistol. It fires only once. Yet once is enough. Even Queen Hexima cannot survive its fury. It is not a weapon. It is the last word.

The Lumex

—A raven staff forged from obsidian and dreamspun bone. It reveals fears. Bends reality. Carries the weight of grief and vision alike.

Haley, the Athame hath spoken.

Thou art chosen—not for strength, nor for might, but for the balance of the Fates... Light and Shadow.

It shall find evil, point the way, and, when the hour is dire, fly to destroy it.

The Athame chooses once. And once only.

Fail her... and she will bury herself in your bones.

"Ok—ay," Riya said slowly. "That's enough terrifying knife fantasy for one night."

She turned to Haley, a flicker of alarm in her eyes.

"Hales—Put that thing down. Slowly."

But Haley didn't.

Instead, she flipped it over and the Athame spun through the air like an eager puppy and landed back in her palm with a shimmer.

"Aww," Haley cooed. "Cute. It likes me."

"Yay," Riya deadpanned. "A knife liking you is not a meet-cute."

She could already tell this was a losing battle, so she turned to something she *could* control—her own weapon.

"Inky," Riya muttered, "where's mine? Don't I get a... I don't know... a stabby souvenir?"

Inky responded in looping script.

Yes. You may take from what remains.
Yet when your true power wakes... You may find no weapon is needed.

Riya sighed. "Fine. I'll take the Lumex. It's creepy, but manageable. Haley can be the killer in the family."

"Hey! I'm not a killer!"

"The knife thinks otherwise," Riya teased.

Suddenly, the hidden door creaked and spun open behind them. A second later, the first blue door blew wide, as if some unseen force had flung it.

Inky snapped shut with a sharp *thwap.*

Riya grabbed the Lumex and Inky. Haley tucked the Athame into her waistband and swiped the velvet box in one motion.

No words. Just instinct.

They bolted up the stairs, breath ragged, feet pounding two steps at a time.

The moment they reached the top—back in Haley's house, back where it should've been safe—

SLAM.

The trapdoor snapped shut behind them, sealing with a sharp hiss like it had never been open at all.

They barely had time to process before a sudden *whirring* sound made them both freeze.

The Athame hit the floor and spun hard, the blade flashing as it twirled—wild and erratic, like a compass losing its mind.

Then—without warning—it shot across the room in a blur of lightning. THWACK.

It buried itself deep in the wall, quivering. Pointing straight at Audrey and

Sarah's house across the street.

A thin black gash spread from the impact site.

And then...it bled.

Thick, tar-like ooze began to trickle from the crack in the drywall, slow at first, then steadily leaking like a wound that had been waiting years to open.

Riya backed up. "Um... why is the wall bleeding? Tar? Or bleeding at all?!" She blinked, nose wrinkling.

"Gross. Nope. We're not unpacking that right now."

She marched forward with false confidence.

"Just grab it and go. That knife is way too creepy."

Haley picked it up. Fresh words were etching themselves across the handle, glowing pink as they carved into the glass like living light.

She who bears the Athame shall stand against the Shadow Gloze, and their clash shall be unto death.

Haley's face dropped.

"Ray... the knife says I have to fight that gross-smelling ogre from the kitchen."

"No."

"Yes."

Riya gulped. "Maybe it's just... metaphorical?"

Not waiting for an answer, she hefted the Lumex up the stairs.

The middle step let out an extra-loud *creeaaak*, like it wasn't buying that theory either.

At the top, Haley's bedroom door swung open on its own.

Riya marched in, chucked the Lumex into the closet, Inky on the bed, and collapsed next to it with a dramatic sigh.

"Okay, Hales, I'm ready to find out what happened to our moms at the Door of Bones."

But then—a *hiss* echoed from the kitchen.

Riya stiffened. "What was that?"

"Probably just the stairs settling," Haley shrugged.

But if they'd stayed downstairs one second longer, they would've seen the truth.

The front door—still unlocked from the Malum sisters' earlier ambush—gave a slow, aching creak.

And through the gap, a Shiverskin lunged inside—wet, snarling, hungry for something it couldn't yet have.

It hurled its skin suit onto the hidden lever beneath the railing—like it had known it was there all along—snapped it down with a vicious yank, and vanished under the stairs.

100

The steps sealed shut above its rotting head, closing slow and heavy, like a train of terror grinding in the dark.

The light flickered once, twice—and in that split second, two beady black eyes and a flash of yellow fangs disappeared into the darkness.

CHAPTER TWENTY-ONE

Two Days Before Halloween

FROM: INKY
TO: RIYA & HALEY

Your mothers had nothing to smile about—

They'd faced death twice in a single night. First, when the Vespergate. Second, when the Door of Bones swallowed them whole.

But somehow—

A glowing red arch swam into view through the haze. They had never heard of a *second door*. And this one looked like the entrance to hell.

Its fall-colored flames—deep oranges, furious reds—licked up the walls in a demonic dance, casting warped shadows that pulsed with heat. The air thickened, the temperature rising by the second.

Celeste stopped, sweat trickling down her temple.

"This feels like a trap."

Then—

A new stench slithered in—thick, unmistakable. The sour reek of decay, tangled with the acrid bite of burning hair.

Ten Shiverskins slithered out from behind the nightmarish curtain of darkness—cockroach-like and cold-eyed.

One snarled—then echoed the last words its victim had spoken.

"Fester... fester... nevermore."

But before the Shiverskin could strike—

"That won't be necessary."

A voice rang out—low, commanding, and unmistakably feminine.

Who faced them haunted their every nightmare—it was Queen Hexima.

She looked like a nightmare dragged from the Shadows—skin pale as piano keys, eyes like frozen violets, lips bruised and wine-dark.

Her black hair spiraled around a jagged crown of bones, and her pantsuit—once regal, now torn and trailing like thunderclouds—floated as if the air itself bowed to her.

"I've been waiting," she purred, her grin sharp and cruel. "Ama Lightwice's daughters. So much potential... and now, so deliciously corrupted."

Her smile sharpened into something wicked.

"Join me... and all shall be yours. Fame to drown the stars. Power to break the sky. A world that will crawl, trembling, to kiss your feet."

Her grin darkened.

"Refuse... and I'll take it all."

She raised her hands. Purple-colored lightning cracked through the air—then *boom*.

A jagged cage of searing violet light slammed down around Celeste.

"NO!" Raven screamed.

Queen Hexima's gaze sharpened. "This is between you and me now. You're changing, Raven. You feel it, don't you? The Shadow growing inside you."

Raven's body seized, every muscle locking tight. Her breath hitched, shallow and sharp.

Then—

Her fingernails stretched—slow, unnatural—shaping into razor talons. Silver-gray dust drifted from them, fine as ash, glittering like coffin dust.

"You don't have to fight it," Queen Hexima coaxed, her voice syrupy-sweet and venom-laced. "I could be the mother you never had."

Raven's jaw tightened. Her eyes burned.

"I have a mother," she snapped. "And she's nothing like you!"

With a snarl, Queen Hexima flung her arms upward.

Purple flames spiraled from her palms—twisting, alive—and shot across the room with a deafening hiss.

Then it happened. Raven's hand shot up—instinct, not thought—and she *caught* the orb.

Queen Hexima's smirk faltered.

"No... no, that's—" she hissed, eyes darting over Raven like she could unravel her with a single stare. "That's... impossible. No daughter of a Light Trapper survives my wrath. You should be dust... You should be nothing!"

Raven didn't flinch. Her voice cut through the madness, low and clear.

"Maybe I'm not *just* a Light Trapper anymore."

And then—

CRACK.

A bolt of lightning split the chamber—raw and violent. An eight-pointed star seared itself into Queen Hexima's chest, burning through her decaying skin in blinding gold.

Then, Celeste stepped forward. Free at last.

Her fingers rose like twin pillars of judgment, her voice clear, firm, and echoing with power.

> *Brand thee once, brand thee twice,*
> *Eight-pointed star—eternal price.*
> *In flesh it burns, in shadow glows,*
> *Reveals the sin the spirit knows.*
> *Should treachery or crime draw nigh,*
> *The mark shall blaze—and thou shalt die.*

The star flared. Hexima's body convulsed.

Raven stepped forward, voice ringing with power.

"Be gone, Hexima! Do one good deed a year—"

Her eyes blazed.

"Or join your precious pets in hell."

Queen Hexima's scream split into smoke—then she vanished.

Silence.

Celeste and Raven barely had time to brush the witch's ash from their sleeves before a whirling tunnel seized them—ripping them apart, slamming them back together, and hurling them into a brutal crash beside the Rede.

Ms. Haute lunged. Celeste and Raven flinched, bracing for impact.

A beat. Instead... praise.

"We are *so* proud of you two!" Ms. Haute exclaimed, sweeping them into a dramatic hug. Her perfume hit like a rose explosion.

Ms. Treewith rolled her eyes and gave them each a light swat on the back of the head.

"Enough coddling," she muttered. Her tone dropped like a trapdoor. "Celeste. Raven. You both refused Queen Hexima's offer to join the Shadow Veil. That's why the Door of Bones let you go unharmed."

Mr. Seacoal crossed his arms. "She tempted you with power. You turned her down. That's loyalty."

Raven wanted to scream. *Of course, we turned Hexima down!*

But something caught her eye.

"Uh... Celeste. Your hair," Raven whispered.

Celeste looked down. The tips of her waves were turning a shade of ice

105

white.

She gasped, clutching a strand. "What's happening to my hair?! It looks like enchanted kitten paws or something!"

Then she squinted at Raven. "Wait... your eye. Your left one—it's blue. Like, icy."

"WHAT?!" Raven yelped, digging a small black hand mirror out of her purse. "You've gotta be kidding me!"

Raven yanked her hair to the side, eyes wide. "Check my neck. It's burning like something's being carved into it or cursed or... I don't know. Just look."

Celeste gently swept Raven's hair aside—then gasped. "There's a mark. A triangle with three jagged lines running through it... just like the cover of *The Book of Fates.*"

Raven's fingers flew to the spot, brushing the raised scar. It throbbed beneath her touch, faintly glowing.

"What does it mean?" she whispered, her voice cracking like ice. "Why us?"

Ms. Treewith stepped in, her tone clipped and unreadable.

"It's a warning. You've wandered too close to the edge. And the Shadow Veil has started to notice—both of you."

Raven's breath caught. "So... we're cursed?!"

"No," Ms. Haute said gently. Then, coolly, as her hand slipped into her sleeve. She drew out two necklaces, their surfaces glinting with a quiet, coiled power.

Celeste held a canary-yellow diamond that sparkled like bottled sunlight. Raven's was darker—a black annex stone that shimmered like ink caught mid-spell.

"These are your amulets," Ms. Haute said. "You're part of us now. Like your mother and father, Ama and Henry Lightwice. Use them wisely."

But Raven wasn't so sure because she heard something: a whisper, then a shout.

RUN, RAVEN.

She seized Celeste's arm. "We have to move. What if the spell— I don't know—fries me? My Shadow side—"

"You think you'll explode?"

"Uh, yeah."

"Gross, Raven! Just go."

The instant the clock struck midnight, Raven bolted—but pain detonated at her temples and poured down her spine, molten and blinding.

She clutched for Celeste, fingers slipping on her silk sleeves, her body folding fast.

"Rae—no—what's happening—" Celeste's scream fractured as the aisle erupted with motion.

Two men were already moving. Not rushing. Arriving. As if the moment had been named for them long before it struck.

Hive amulets swung at their throats, pendulums of dark metal, catching the violet spill of moonlight as they closed the distance in three clean strides.

Raven's vision tunneled. The floor surged up.

She never reached it.

Arms caught her—sure, unstartled—lifting her from collapse with practiced ease, as though her fall had always been expected and always his to intercept.

"I'm Xavier," he said, steadying her. "This is my brother, Manchester." A faint smile moved across his mouth. "The Rede claimed we'd meet the most beautiful women in the universe tonight—our forever vitals. Our twin flames."

He blinked once, slow and certain, the expression unfolding across his face like light cresting a horizon. "They were right."

His gaze settled on Raven. "You are the most beautiful woman I've ever seen."

For a suspended second, she forgot her own name. His eyes held depth she had no language for—galaxies turning beneath stillness, heat threaded through calm. Her pulse misstepped. She became acutely aware of his hands at her waist, of how easily he held her, as if gravity had briefly renegotiated itself.

"I—" Raven's voice failed and returned softer. "You catch strangers often?"

"Only the important ones," he said.

A breath of laughter escaped her before she could stop it. She didn't move away. Neither did he.

Across the aisle, Celeste and Manchester stood locked in a quieter collision—no words, just recognition passing between them in widening rings. Celeste's fingers still hovered near his sleeve, as if she'd reached without knowing she had. Manchester watched her like a man who had finally located something lost before memory.

Above them, the moon burned an impossible purple, light pooling along the windows like spilled wine.

Raven felt it then—that subtle, irreversible tilt. Not love. Not yet. But the unmistakable sense of a door opening somewhere inside the world.

One thing was certain—whatever came next would rewrite everything they thought they knew.

CHAPTER TWENTY-TWO

Two Days Before Halloween

Haley wrestled with her stampeding heart, thrashing against her ribs like a wild thing in a cage—furious, frantic, desperate to escape. She couldn't remember it ever skipping three beats in a row. Maybe never.

Her mom had beaten Hexima with Shadow magic... a curse. Magic that slithered. Magic that cut. Magic that never asked permission.

If that's what lived in her blood, no wonder her skin crawled. She reached out and tapped Riya's knee—bony, solid, real.

"I don't feel so well," she whispered.

She let out a shaky breath.

"I mean—yeah, my mom saved yours, but she had to go full cursed mode to do it." Haley fiddled with her sleeve. "What if I'm, like... genetically evil?"

Riya didn't even flinch. "Maybe you're overreacting."

Haley shot her a look.

"I'm just saying," Riya added, casually, "this might be more about Inky than your mom."

"How do you mean?" Haley asked, narrowing her eyes as she suspiciously scooted away from Inky—just in case it was eavesdropping.

"I mean, it skips all the major stuff," Riya said. "Like, how did your mom even get strong enough to curse Hexima? That's not some overnight, light-a-candle-and-make-a-wish kind of magic."

"Ugh, Inky is *so* keeping secrets," Haley groaned.

Inky flipped to a new page and groaned like creaky old knees on stair day.

Dusk draws near—the hour most fitting for study. But first, you must take sustenance.

Dearest Riya, prepare a meal for yourself and Haley. When you return, we shall continue.

"Finally," Riya purred. "You could probably hear my stomach from Dahmorte."

She bounded downstairs.

Haley reached to close Inky, but it jerked and wrote something meant only for her.

I would not speak this before Riya—so I bade her depart.
Haley, within you coils more Shadow than your mother ever carried. Draw too near to evil, and it will claim you.
Tell Riya nothing.
Her gloaming must come first—before you dare test your power—for if it does not, Queen Hexima's curse will unmake her the instant yours awakens.

Just then, the door swung open. Riya beamed, holding two sandwiches.

Haley waved her hand over the book, as if swatting a fly. "Whoa. That was fast."

Riya grinned. "Yeah, well... I'm starving. And I kinda like this new you—thinking things through, trying to study up. Who even are you?"

Inky went blank just in time, and Haley let out a relieved sigh.

Riya rambled mid-bite. "Okay, not to say I told you so—but I totally told you so. We should've had a plan. Now you might be kinda wicked... but we'll figure it out."

Haley nibbled her sandwich.

If Riya knew the whole truth, she'd probably toss hers out the window and run.

"I mean, I like this new side of you..." Riya giggled. "But I also kind of wanna talk about my feelings."

Haley groaned. "Oh no."

"I feel... weirdly invincible," Riya admitted. "Like... confident. Like Axel on the tennis team." Her eyes lit with a spark.

"Ugh. Axel... Griffith?" Haley asked, already regretting it.

"Yeah. Axel. With the black wavy hair and those green eyes that tilt like... trouble."

Haley rolled her eyes, but a smirk tugged at her lips. "Okay, fine. I'll bite. Axel's a solid pick."

110

Riya grinned. "Maybe I'll ask him out when we get back to school."

"You'd ask him out?" Haley raised a brow.

"Why not? And what about you and Hayes?" Riya shot back.

Haley blushed.

Riya's grin widened. "You know—Hayes Harper from your physics class? Long blond hair, baseball team, six-pack situation, and those tragically dorky copper glasses?"

"Can we not?" Haley muttered, rubbing her forehead. "My temples are pounding like I wasn't invited to my own brain party."

"Probably just tired," Riya said, though she wasn't so sure.

Haley's stomach twisted.

She wanted to enjoy this break from magic trauma talk—laugh about crushes, pretend things were normal—but the fear clung to her like humidity she couldn't shake.

"I'd like to talk about... uh, stuff," Haley muttered. "But we should probably start your gloaming. Like... now."

Riya blinked. "What?"

"I mean it. Let's force Inky to do your gloaming like, five minutes ago."

Riya raised a brow. "Okay, something's up. Did Inky say something while I was gone?"

Haley froze. Lying to Riya felt like trying to bottle a hurricane. But she had to.

She shoved Inky toward her. "Here. You take Inky."

Riya frowned. Haley never gave it up that easily. This meant something.

Her clammy palms left damp prints on Inky's leather cover. Its lone eye blinked, squinting like it was stung with salt—though Riya didn't notice. She was too tangled in the moment, too locked on Haley.

Haley kept flicking glances at her phone like it held the meaning of life.

"Why do you keep checking your phone—like you're waiting for a crush to text?" Riya asked, her side-eye sharp.

"I'm not," Haley muttered. "I just want to get to the next part. So you can finally get your powers."

Riya narrowed her eyes. Something was off with Haley. But before she could press, Inky's pages fluttered forward, dragging her attention back.

It still hadn't said what gloaming would actually feel like. Riya just hoped it would be easy—like flipping a switch.

Because with less than forty-eight hours left to recharge their powers, every second was slipping away.

CHAPTER TWENTY-THREE

Two Days Before Halloween

A groaning creak, then a sharp click, drifted up the stairs to Haley's room—like the house had just unlocked a bank vault.

Riya's head snapped toward the hallway, eyes wide. "What was that?"

Inky slammed shut, caught mid-confession, its leather hot against her palms.

A draft slithered in beneath the door, carrying the faint bite of night air. From downstairs came the muffled rise and fall of their parents' voices at the front door.

Riya checked her phone—**7:00 p.m.**

"Ugh, Hales..." Riya groaned. "My parents are here too."

Haley froze. "We're still in our PJs," she hissed. "What do we do? We need a whole day to finish your gloaming. You think they'll actually let us stay home again?"

Riya swallowed hard. "Maybe... if we fake being sick." Her voice wavered, like even she didn't believe it.

They tiptoed downstairs and immediately heard Haley's dad booming from the kitchen.

"Wow, you girls sure made a mess in here! Weren't you supposed to be sick? Looks more like a party."

The cousins winced.

The kitchen was wrecked—cereal bowls on the floor, sandwich fixings everywhere, like a deli had exploded.

Riya instantly regretted skipping clean-up.

They turned the corner slowly, guilt practically glowing off them like neon signs that screamed—*Busted*.

Riya tugged at her sleeve, eyes locked on the floor.

Haley tried to act casual, but her poker face was cracked—eyebrows raised a little too high, smile a little too tight.

"Fake a cough," Haley whispered.

"You fake a cough."

Too late.

The judgment was already in full swing.

Raven and Celeste exchanged a glance sharp enough to cut glass.

It said, *Try again.*

Manchester strode across the kitchen, his legs moving as if on a conveyor belt—smooth, fast, unstoppable. He pressed a warm hand to Riya's forehead, eyes narrowing.

"No fever," he said, voice tinged with suspicion. "And making a mess at Haley's? That's not like you, Ray."

Riya shrugged, forcing a tired smile. "Yeah, I know. I guess I'm more out of it than I thought."

"Riya could stay another night," Haley cut in. "At least until Halloween. She can rest—and help me clean up."

"Hmmm, I don't know..." Celeste said, arms folded. "You don't want to wear out your welcome."

"But she wants to stay. Right, Ray?" Haley nudged her.

Riya didn't answer. She just grabbed a sponge and started scrubbing cereal off the tile.

Their parents traded a loaded glance, then slipped out of the room.

Haley leaned in and whispered, "Think it worked?"

Riya shook her head, eyes still on the hallway where their parents had disappeared. "Not even close," she murmured. "My dad knows. He always knows."

She sank onto the edge of the counter, defeated. "Both our dads are doctors, remember? They can smell fake symptoms in their sleep."

Haley flopped down beside her with a groan.

"Great. Busted and grounded before we even save the world."

She punched the air.

"We're out here trying to keep the universe from imploding, and our ultimate nemesis is... parental supervision." She threw herself back like a tragic heroine, arms spread wide.

Riya cracked a tired smile.

"Pretty sure Inky forgot a chapter: beware dads with medical degrees.

They can diagnose strep throat *and* questionable life choices."

Mom-heels clicked back in—sharp and fast.

"One question," Celeste said. "Are you really sick, or is this about decorating for your birthday party?"

Riya froze.

The sponge dropped with a wet *splat.*

Haley caught the panic flash in Riya's eyes.

"Nope. Absolutely not," she cut in. "Party's a maybe. People flake, plans change—immaturity, or whatever." She shrugged. "We just need more time to get better."

Then, fast—like speed-running an alibi—"Homework's done. No tests. We'll clean it all up tomorrow. Promise."

Celeste circled them, her long hair—ice white tips—swinging like a cat's tail dipped in milk.

"So this has nothing to do with the teasing at school?"

Neither cousin had spared a thought for Audrey and Sarah in days. Family secrets had a way of shrinking mean girls—until they felt small enough to be irrelevant.

Their parents eyed them like detectives.

"No, nothing like that. Honest," Haley said, stepping into the light. Her confidence sparkled, like she'd just won a tiny courtroom battle.

Her mom gave a slow nod. "Okay... well. We ordered pizza. Should be here any minute and—"

Clatter.

A broom toppled behind the laundry machine. The *open-broom-moto...*

The room froze.

Even the old wall heater went silent, as if it didn't dare interrupt.

Celeste narrowed her eyes, scanning the cousins' faces like a shark scenting blood. "Wait," she said slowly. "Is there something you want to tell us?"

The broom stayed still—but the question lingered, heavy as a spell left hanging.

"Seems like there is," Manchester said, his voice low. "That only happens when someone's hiding something."

The cousins felt exposed. Plastic wrap transparent.

But honestly? Their parents weren't innocent either.

They'd hidden world-tilting truths—big enough to split a lifetime in two. Secrets that rewrote memories, blurred childhood into betrayal, and left questions echoing in the hollow between heartbeats.

Silence thickened around them, heavy as wet wool.

And then—

Ding-dong.

The doorbell snapped the moment in half.

The cousins exchanged a glance—tight, knowing, wordless—and bolted upstairs like the truth might chase them if they stayed one second longer.

Their footsteps thudded up the stairs in sync with their pounding hearts.

And behind them, the smell of greasy, golden cheese drifted in, a bribe wrapped in garlic crust.

But comfort wasn't enough.

Not anymore.

CHAPTER TWENTY-FOUR

Two Days Before Halloween

Riya flopped onto the bed with a huff. "That was close."

"Yeah. But we had to lie," Haley said. "We've got like, what, thirty hours left to finish your gloaming?"

The door creaked open.

Riya snatched Inky and stuffed it under the covers. Their moms came in with pizza and lemon water.

"Peace offering," said Raven, handing over the plates.

"Thanks, Mom," Haley said, eyes locked on the gooey cheese.

"We're testing you," Raven added. "To see if you can stay out of trouble."

Riya took the first glorious bite of cheesy goodness and nearly forgot herself—nearly unraveled every secret Inky had spilled with a single slip.

"You can trust us," she said, shifting just enough to block Inky from view. "Because, you know... You don't know unless you try. Kind of like Wayki—"

Haley's elbow nailed her in the ribs. Hard.

Celeste's brow arched. "Sounded like you were about to say something... a word..."

"Nope. Just hungry," Riya said fast. "We say weird stuff when we're starving. It's a medical condition."

It worked.

Their moms kissed their foreheads and left the room.

"Phew," Riya said, grabbing her pizza. "I almost blew it."

"Yeah. From now on, I do the talking. You chew."

Riya perked up when she snagged a garlic knot. "Yes. It has, like, a whole piece of—"

She froze, the thought hitting mid-bite, cutting through her brief bubble of happiness.

"You realize Inky skipped over the day we showed up?" she said, flopping back on the bed. "Our grand baby debut. You'd think that would've made the highlight reel by now."

"I'm sure it's gearing up," Haley said through a mouthful. "It's probably when that old hag cursed us or something."

As if on cue, Inky snapped open to a fresh page. This time it wasn't just eager—it was ravenous.

Not only did it love to scare them, it seemed to relish dropping truths sharp enough to cut the bond they held so dear.

CHAPTER TWENTY-FIVE

Two Days Before Halloween

FROM: INKY
TO: RIYA & HALEY

So, we begin...

Hear now of the night you were born—A night steeped in shadow and split-second fate. A night that unmade the world you should have known.

You were taken. By her. *Queen Hexima.*

And while the curse sealed itself in silence, Manchester drove like he was racing the Fates, his grip tightening as the Jeep tore around each curve in the road.

Celeste and Raven clung to their seatbelts—bodies wrecked from labor, faces streaked with sweat and tears.

Their arms were empty.

Their babies were gone.

Stolen.

And they knew exactly by whom.

But first—they needed reinforcements.

"Hell-ooo! You home?" Celeste barked, storming her parents' porch like a soldier back from war.

Inside, Raven shoved the door open. "Mom. DAD?"

But the second they stepped in—everything went still.

The air was wrong. Too sweet. Too rotten.

Like melted birthday candles and something festering underneath.

Celeste pressed against the wall. "That smell..."

"Elementals," Raven muttered, her voice tight. "Mom—help. Our babies are... gone. Hexima took them!"

"How?" Ama snapped, her voice sharp as glass. "The protection spell was ironclad."

Then she stopped. Her face went pale—blue eyes wide, breath caught.

"The curse," she whispered. "The eight-pointed star..."

Celeste nodded. "It forced her to do one good deed a year. That sliver of goodness... was just enough."

A loophole the evil witch had long hungered for—her chance to consume even more light.

The room erupted—potions slammed from cabinets, spells shouted, chaos mounting—

Until a knock at the door froze them all.

Ama opened it.

And there she was. *Queen Hexima*—looking every bit the nightmare they remembered—only worse.

In her crooked hands—shaped for cursing rather than any gentle touch—rested the horror Celeste and Raven had prayed would never come to pass.

Two blackberry-swaddled infants slept soundlessly in her arms—held with a twisted mockery of maternal grace, as if she savored the theft of what was never hers to claim.

On either side of her stood a Shiverskin—hulking, motionless, their matted fur slick with shadow.

Queen Hexima's smile widened, slow and cold.

"Miss me?" she purred.

Raven lunged forward. "Touch them and I'll end you!"

"Don't cross the threshold!" Ama shouted. "She can't come in and you can't go out!"

Queen Hexima raised a brow, her expression carved from ice.

"Relax," she purred, each syllable dripping like venom from a fang. "I'm not here to fight... I'm here to negotiate."

She lifted you two higher—your tiny bodies, too still, cheeks soft and vulnerable, lashes tangled like spider silk.

A cruel invitation.

"A witch for a witch," she whispered, smile thin as a blade. "Surrender your powers, and I'll loosen my side of the curse. Maybe—just maybe—they'll live long enough to watch the Fates burn."

Her grin widened, inhuman.

"Fair trade... yes?"

Raven's eyes narrowed. "Tell us how to break it without giving you anything."

Queen Hexima's smile twisted.

124

"One must die." Hexima's gaze slid to Raven, unblinking. "And the other?"

"She's the one who must deliver the blow."

Snap.

Queen Hexima's pointed boots struck the welcome mat, grinding in the dirt of darker realms.

"Here... let me show you how it's done."

A curse bled from her touch—deep as marrow, binding as a bloodline—so absolute no witch, no star, no heaven or hell could unmake it.

And then—without hurry—she stepped inside. Fully. Smugly.

Breaking every sacred law of witchcraft that the Lightwices had ever known.

That was all the invitation Celeste and Raven needed. They did not hesitate.

Together, they unleashed the Banishing Spell. Light erupted through the ceiling—violent, searing—like the night sky itself was being torn in two.

The walls trembled. Shadows flailed.

First, a swirling green mist curled around you both, lifting gently before dropping you into your mother's waiting arms.

Then came the blast—blinding, merciless—swallowing Queen Hexima and her cursed pets whole. It roared like tires screaming across wet asphalt.

And then—they were gone.

Or so they thought.

The air still carried the aftertaste of Queen Hexima's presence—bitter, metallic, a warning that the story was far from over.

Far below, in a sliver of Dahmorte deeper than death, her spirit curled in on itself.

Watching.

Waiting... *For you two.*

CHAPTER TWENTY-SIX

TWO DAYS BEFORE HALLOWEEN

Riya let out a shaky breath. "So you were right. Like, so right," she huffed. "Hexima cursed us at birth. And now I wish I'd never asked."

Haley cracked a tired grin, though real fear knotted underneath. "We've faced worse. Probably."

Without warning, Riya grabbed the nearest pillow, screamed into it like it owed her money, then collapsed backward, arms sprawled, eyes locked on the ceiling.

Finally, she cracked the silence. "No, I don't think we've faced anything this bad. This isn't a pop quiz, Hales—it's curses and potential blood loss, and... what if we fail?"

Haley didn't flinch. "We won't. Failing's not on the menu."

They sat in silence, both mulling over what *failure* really meant. It used to be throwing a mediocre party or bombing a chem test.

Now it meant the world ending. Their family erased. Their home literally burning to the ground.

Riya sat up straighter, and that alone made Haley nervous.

"Look, I don't know if I can just... blindly do this anymore," Riya said. "Can't we just rewind all of it?"

Haley tilted her head, catching the glow of the oversized moon.

"I wouldn't trade it," she said softly. "Figuring this out—" she gestured between them—"what we are—it's changed everything. For once, we have answers. And... haven't you always wanted a sense of purpose?"

"Yes," Riya admitted with a hiss. Then, quieter: "I guess. but—"

Whap.

Suddenly, Inky snapped shut.

Riya jumped. "Uh... Hales?"

"Yeah?"

"Tell me that was just super weird timing."

Haley eyed the book's sealed spine. "Nope."

Riya swallowed hard. "So... plan B?"

"Plan B," Haley echoed, her voice turning steel-cold.

She looked up.

"How to kill Hexima—without either of us dying."

"I don't even know if that's possible..." Riya murmured, her voice trailing like smoke in a collapsing room.

"I do," Haley said, placing the pillow behind her back. "She's been hunting us since day one, and now I want to know why."

Haley tapped the book like she was knocking on a tiny door, trying to wake it up. Its slit of an eye just slid shut—like it had decided to nap instead.

"It'd be nice to actually know what Hexima wants with us," Haley muttered, heat creeping into her voice at Inky.

Riya opened her mouth, then shut it again, pulling a goldfish frown. She glanced at her phone—the night-light had shifted to amber glow mode.

"Whoa. Is it seriously that late?" she asked, blinking.

Haley nodded.

They should've been exhausted after a full day of secrets, near breakdowns, and cosmic revelations.

But they were buzzing—wired from adrenaline and ancient truths.

Riya tugged the comforter up to her chin. "I mean, if we ignore the whole stabby destiny thing for a sec, it's kinda great—you can astral project, I've got Chemisource. Worst case, you get grounded, just float over to my place."

Haley buried her face in a pillow. "Sure. Straight through the Door of Bones. That won't backfire at all."

Then she snapped upright—back rigid, eyes wide—like a puppy begging for a treat.

"I have an idea," she blurted. "It kinda goes with your gloaming—oh, and you going first." Her voice chimed like a broken alarm clock, a little too bright, a little too sly.

Before Riya could shut it down, Haley curled her knees to her chest. A slow, sinister smile spread across her face.

The lamplight caught Haley's eyes, and for a heartbeat, Riya swore she saw them darken—blackberry-colored ripples swallowing the hazel until nothing but black remained.

128

A blink later, it was gone.

CHAPTER TWENTY-SEVEN

Two Days Before Halloween

Outside, the wind clawed at the shutters, each groan of the house making Riya glance toward the hallway.

Haley was still staring at nothing, lips curved like she'd just heard a secret the universe hadn't meant for her.

Riya hugged her knees. "Okay, so... you're giving me creepy movie-villain vibes right now."

Haley's gaze snapped back, warm again, calm even. "Relax. Just thinking."

Her voice carried weight—low, steady, almost too steady. "You should test your powers first," she said, eyes glinting with something Riya couldn't place. "Like we'll do your gloaming."

Riya went quiet.

"I don't want to use my powers. And especially not... my gloaming," she finally admitted.

Haley's heart skipped. If Riya didn't try tonight, it could already be too late.

But then Riya leaned in, her voice soft but steady.

"Think about it. You should go first. You can help our moms, test your powers, and prove you're still Light like me. Triple win."

She said it like a joke, but the words hung heavier than she meant. In the back of her mind, "testing" Haley's powers felt a lot like striking a match just to see how fast the room would burn.

Haley wrinkled her nose. "No. Bad idea."

But she didn't move.

131

"I wouldn't even know how to start, Ray."

"Inky said your mom focused hard on where she wanted to go. Try that," Riya urged.

"It'll be quick," she added, her voice dropping to a whisper. "Inky won't even know. Our moms are acting totally off—and they didn't even decorate for Halloween. We need to help."

Haley hesitated, fingers twitching, but beneath the fear burned that wildfire spark that always pushed her to risk, to leap, to touch the flame.

"I hate that I'm considering this," she muttered.

But she was.

Haley drew in a shaky breath, and nodded. Against her better judgment, she split.

"Okay. Let's do it."

And before she could snatch the words back—before the unseen Shadow force waiting for her wild side to wreck five thousand years of prophecy—Haley didn't think. Instinct took over.

She locked in, heart pounding, as the air crackled sharp and charged around her, like a soda can seconds from bursting.

Then—WHAM.

The world spun.

She turned just long enough to see her body slumped on the bed, eyes wide and blank. A golden cord shimmered from her chest, tethering spirit to flesh like a glowing thread of breath.

Then—ZAP.

She shot through the sky, past rooftops and stars, until a swampy forest yawed open beneath her—drenched, creepy, and smelling like gym socks left in a haunted drawer.

A black castle rose from the trees like a wound. No moat. No guards. Just fangs of stone beneath a haunted lavender moon.

Something yanked her upward, dragging her to the tallest window.

Inside, a waxy face turned—lavender eyes glowing, glassy, dead.

Hexima.

Her name hit like a curse.

And then—

"COME HERE, HALEY!"

The shriek was sharp, jagged, inhuman.

Hexima lunged, right through the window. The glass didn't even crack—she slipped through like smoke through teeth.

Haley grabbed the glowing golden thread—and yanked.

Nothing.

Her chest tightened. She yanked again. Harder. Still nothing.

Inches from her nose—perched on the windowsill like a cursed cat—Hexima hissed, her voice curling into Haley's ear like cold mist.

"I wonder... how long you'll scream before you beg to join me."

Haley's pulse roared. Her fingers slipped.

Yank. Yank. YANK.

The cord held firm. She was stuck. Trapped between body and Shadow. And Hexima was almost on her.

Haley squeezed her eyes shut.

Think. Think.

Her room—

Riya's voice.

Her bed.

Home.

NOW.

POP.

Haley slammed back into her body like a car crash in reverse.

Air punched from her lungs. Her eyes flew open. Everything was spinning. She was back. But not alone.

Riya was mid-freak-out. "Your eyes went white! You froze! And this glowing rope was wrapped around you!"

Haley gasped. "I think she saw me. She was in some cursed candle circle, and she just—reached through the glass like it wasn't even there."

Riya's face went pale. "Who? WHAT?"

"I think Hexima..."

The lights flickered. The room filled with the scent of blown-out candles.

"Do you smell that?" Haley whispered.

Too late.

Invisible hands gripped her throat. Haley choked, writhing as cold claws burrowed beneath her skin.

Her eyes rolled back. Her body seized.

"HALEY!" Riya screamed, grabbing Inky.

Haley's body jolted, her face draining to gray. Her eyes turned ink-black—bottomless, unnatural.

"LEAVE HALEY ALONE, YOU MONSTER!" Riya shouted, hoisting Inky like it was a medieval frying pan.

The book glowed.

The Shadow shrieked—high and ragged—like an angry cat getting a surprise bath, then hurled itself backward, screeching out the window in a blur of smoke and hate.

Riya's heart pounded like it was trying to escape her chest. She blinked, stunned. "Wait... did I just vaporize a demon with Inky?" she asked, shaky.

Haley coughed, her voice raw and trembling. "That... was *so* not okay. That thing made me see something—a future, I think—but it was all twisted. I was *her*."

She shivered.

"Her, as in Hexima, her. Like I was her creepy little pet or something. No thoughts, no feelings...and—"

She gulped hard, eyes wide.

"No soul."

Riya let out a sob—half horror, half exhaustion. "Not good! You are never using your powers again. Ever!"

Haley winced. "But you saved me. You used your Chemisource powers!"

"I think it was Inky," Riya said, collapsing beside her. "Do you think she... came back with you?"

The only answer was a sharp scrape across the window.

They froze.

Outside, Hexima's ghostly form hovered in the dark, one twisted claw dragging slowly down the glass—then vanishing in a flash of purple dust.

She was coming.

And this time, not even sunrise would save them.

CHAPTER TWENTY-EIGHT

ONE DAY BEFORE HALLOWEEN

Morning crept in with a burnt orange glow, moving across Haley's bed like spilled tea.

Riya blinked awake, puffy-eyed and aching, every limb heavy with the weight of too much truth.

Haley groaned beside her, one arm draped off the bed like she'd been wrung out and forgotten.

Neither of them had really slept.

"Did you dream anything?" Riya asked, her voice cracked and thin.

Haley shook her head. "No. Just... cold. Like something was watching me all night."

Riya sat up slowly, rubbing her temples as the pounding in her head eased. The room felt off. Too quiet.

She glanced around—and froze.

Inky was gone.

She groaned, her stomach twisting. "Great. Cue the paranoia. What if your mom has it? Just sitting there, waiting to unleash full-mom-terror on our already fragile souls?"

Haley shot upright, eyes wide. "No. Absolutely not. My mom couldn't hide something like that. She'd have kicked down my door like she scored front-row concert tickets—then grounded me for life and banned pizza just to prove a point."

Riya snorted. "Honestly? That's cruel and unusual punishment."

Silence stretched between them.

Riya glanced at the space where Inky used to be.

"So... should we go looking?"

Haley shrugged. "Maybe. Or maybe it'll dive bomb down the stairs like last time, right after our parents leave."

"Fingers crossed," Riya said, but her voice wavered.

Because this time? Something felt different.

By the time they dragged themselves downstairs, Raven was clinging to a coffee mug like it was the only thing keeping her upright.

She set it down just long enough to hack at fruit with sharp, deliberate chops. The bags under her eyes were practically designer.

"Morning, girls," she said, forcing a smile that didn't quite reach her tired eyes.

Haley mumbled a response. Riya stayed quiet.

Raven studied them. "Did you two sleep okay?"

Haley nodded—too fast.

"No nightmares?" Raven asked, knife hovering mid-slice.

"Nope," Haley lied, voice light. Too light.

Raven rolled the knife to one side and squared her shoulders, taking up all the air in the kitchen.

"I'm thinking of closing the shop early today," she said, too casually. "Something feels... off."

Haley and Riya froze.

"I think it's time we talk," she added. "About everything."

Upstairs, a loud *thud-pop-bang* cracked through the ceiling like a ghost bowling strike.

Haley launched into a fake coughing fit. "No, no—we're fine." *Hack, cough.* "Riya's got me covered. You should totally go to work."

Raven narrowed her eyes, clearly unconvinced.

But then—a car honked outside.

"I swear, your father still honks like we're sneaking out to prom," she muttered, grabbing her bag. "Fine. But this conversation's happening. Soon."

She pointed her coffee mug at them like a warning.

Then the door clicked shut.

Riya nodded stiffly like a porcelain doll on the verge of a nervous breakdown. She jabbed Haley hard in the ribs.

"Okay, rise and panic. We need to find Inky—like, now, now."

A loud clang echoed from upstairs. The cousins froze.

"That's not ominous at all," Riya muttered.

They bolted—skipping steps, scrambling up the rickety attic ladder.

And there, right in the middle of the dusty floorboards, sat Inky. Closed and waiting.

"Phew," Haley exhaled, hurrying over. But then she squinted. "Wait... how'd it get up here?"

"It's opened the attic latch before," Riya said flatly. "Maybe it walked itself back."

WHAP.

Haley blinked. "Cool, cool. So the haunted book is moody this morning."

Inky slapped the floor and burst open.

Haley, the projection you did last night was extremely dangerous.

Riya, I am ashamed of you! You should have stopped Haley and been the wiser older cousin!

I was concealed, for your protection.

Last night, Queen Hexima nearly shattered the eight-pointed star curse your mothers sealed in blood and moonlight.

One more crack, and she would have broken free of Everbind—unleashing ruin on the Fates themselves.

But worse, Haley—she followed you here—to the ash realm.

Like a hound catching the scent of your onu, she tracked your spirit back through the Veil.

And she is not alone.

Queen Hexima's line has dwelled among the ashes for centuries—feeding upon their own onus until nothing sacred remained.

Now they rise with a single vow: to finish what she began, and to scour the Lightwices from existence.

Haley leaned in. "Wait... Hexima has family? Here?"

Inky didn't hesitate.

The Malums.

Riya blinked like the words had personally insulted her.

"Like... Audrey and Sarah Malum? Our neighbors? The ones who sparkle in gym class and bake sympathy muffins if you so much as sneeze?"

Yes—Riya—The Malums. They have borne their Shadow through your town for generations untold.

You must not draw near to them. Not until your gloaming is fulfilled. Not until the hour finds you ready.

Riya snorted so hard she nearly choked. "Okay, chill, spooky book.

They're not villains, they're honor roll students with an unhealthy obsession with trends."

Haley crossed her arms. "Yeah, they're like... weirdly perfect. If they're secretly evil, I quit reality."

But Riya stopped cold.

Because deep down—under the snark, beneath the logic—there was something.

A tug.

Just a tiny one. In the pit of her stomach. It happened every time the Malum sisters walked into a room. Like indigestion mixed with déjà vu... and sprinkled with guilt.

Shame.

That's what it was. Not because they were mean—not really.

Audrey always held the door open. Sarah complimented people's outfits as if it were her part-time job.

No, it wasn't *what* they did. It was *how* they made her feel. Like mirrors, she didn't want to look into.

Still, Riya shook her head. Nope. Not doing this. They weren't evil.

They were annoying. Intimidating. Maybe a little too perfect.

But evil? She couldn't go there. Not today.

Besides, Haley going full villain was way more urgent than decoding the mysteries of pastel cardigans and suspicious kindness.

Ding-dong.

The doorbell rang like a death sentence wrapped in a chime.

Riya and Haley froze.

CHAPTER TWENTY-NINE

ONE DAY BEFORE HALLOWEEN

Haley yanked the door open—

Audrey and Sarah stood on the porch like a fashion-forward horror poster, silhouettes framed by gray fog that curled around their pointy heels like smoke from a dying fire.

Their smiles didn't reach their eyes.

"We were just talking about y-you," Haley said, forcing a smile that barely stretched across her face. Her voice cracked on the last word, nervously.

"We know," Audrey said, cold as iced tea on a funeral day. Her paper-blonde hair slipped over one eye like a curtain drawn for drama.

"Sarah and I were thinking of heading into the woods. Swap scary stories, stir up some spooky vibes." She smirked, all faux innocence.
"You in?"

Sarah didn't flinch. She just tilted her head slightly like a doll deciding whether or not to blink.

Haley was halfway out the door before she knew what she was doing. "Um... sure. That sounds... fun... but..."

Riya's hand shot out and clamped around Haley's sleeve like a seatbelt mid-crash.

"Wait," she whispered, locking eyes with Haley. "We're not supposed to leave, remember? Inky just casually dropped the bomb of a lifetime that our perfectly polished neighbors might be—oh, I don't know—monsters. In heels."

She leaned in, voice barely above a breath. "We can't just follow them into the woods like they owe us something."

Audrey tilted her head. "What was that?" she asked sweetly, but her voice had a poisonous edge. She twirled a strand of hair like she was winding a snare. "Scared you'll get caught or something?"

"No!" Riya snapped too quickly. "We're just... sorta grounded. That's all."

Riya's instincts crackled like a busted light socket. She'd never liked the sisters, but after what Inky said, she was officially on high alert for evil wrapped in pastel pink.

Not that she fully believed the book—she was rationally suspicious. That's what kept her safe.

Scratch that. Kept her *and* Haley safe.

Haley, meanwhile, was riding that all-too-familiar rush—the one that smelled like trouble, adventure, and inconvenient truth. This could end up as just a stupid retreat with the Sisters Plague... or the moment Inky proved itself a liar, leaving only her and Riya to trust.

Either way, she was ready to gamble.

Haley spun, flashing a smirk so over-the-top it practically deserved its own spotlight.

"C'mon, Ray. It's just an hour. What could possibly go wrong?"

The house seemed to answer with a low, hollow creak, like the floorboards were holding their breath. Somewhere far off, a door clicked shut all on its own.

"Omg, yes, nothing! Right?" Audrey chirped. "And maybe after, we can, like, totally help you decorate for your party?"

Her voice was frosted in sugar, but something bitter curdled beneath it like cotton candy spun with bile.

Haley moved. Riya didn't. Their eyes met, trading silent messages.

"We're fine on the helping front, seriously," Haley said, her voice fragile, like broken glass.

Audrey crossed her arms and popped her gum—loudly. "Seriously? You two think you can pull off the best party without us?" she said, her tone suddenly flat, like a threat.

Audrey and Sarah never cared about Halloween. Not once. They'd roll their eyes at decorations, skip childish costumes, and mock the candy bowl. Now—suddenly—they were desperate to get inside.

Haley hesitated. She glanced at Riya. Then at the sisters. Then back at the door.

"Yay. I seriously think we'll be fine without your help... but we're always down for spooky stories," she said—too fast, too eager. Her voice cracked, but she covered it with a grin as she yanked their jackets off the hook.

144

Riya stayed rooted, as if the floor had poured itself up around her ankles and hardened to stone.

Her arms hung limp at her sides, fingers twitching like they were still clinging to the edge of sanity. Her eyes flicked toward the attic—toward Inky—then snapped back to Haley.

"Are you serious?" she hissed.

"I know," Haley muttered. "But what if Inky's wrong?"

Riya's voice cracked. "And what if it's not?"

Haley was already halfway out the door, dragging her cousin like a kid hauling a reluctant sibling into a haunted house—right into the whispering woods on the eve of something ancient and very, very wrong.

Still, Riya followed. Because the thought of Haley facing it alone was somehow worse than whatever waited beyond the trees.

The door creaked shut behind them.

And somewhere—maybe in the fog, maybe only in their minds—a whisper curled through the air:

Too late now.

CHAPTER THIRTY

ONE DAY BEFORE HALLOWEEN

The fog thickened, curling around their ankles like smoke from a fire that never died.

Each step into the woods grew heavier, as if the earth itself was trying to pin them in place. Branches clawed down like bony fingers, snagging their sleeves and hair, whispering warnings in a language older than the universe.

Haley glanced back. The house had blurred into the mist like it had never been there at all. Only the porch light remained.

It flickered once. Twice. Then went out. Just like a red flag, giving up.

"No turning back now," Haley whispered.

Riya clutched her arm. "Wait—where are we even going?"

Haley's grin was quick, crooked. "To see if Inky's just dramatic... or if we're walking straight into a horror movie."

"Great," Riya muttered. "Should've worn my *don't-get-murdered* outfit." Her voice cracked as she added, "Inky literally said not to follow them into the woods."

Haley didn't stop, but her voice rose a notch. "I know what Inky said," she muttered. "But I need to know why it hates them so much. Why all the secrets? What are they hiding?"

She glanced back, eyes sharp. "I have to see for myself, okay? Just... stay close."

They hurried after Audrey and Sarah, whose spider-like strides cracked through the underbrush like storks in sticky reeds.

Something was wrong. So wrong. Then, through the haze, they saw it.

147

A clearing yawned open ahead—too round, too precise, like the forest had been holding its breath for this moment.

And at its center... Five blackberry-colored blankets lay in a perfect circle.

Folded. Waiting. Eight tall candles—plum wax dripping in lazy rivulets—stood sentinel around them.

Their flames burned violet-blue, flickering without wind, each one bending inward as if bowing to the blankets.

The morning sun filtered weakly through the mist, sickly and thin.

Riya's skin prickled—like the shadows had fingers, tracing lightly along her arms.

"This feels creepy," she muttered.

"That means it's working," Audrey said, flashing a grin so wicked it could curdle milk.

Riya edged closer. "Why are there *five* blankets? There's only four of us."

"A spooky reminder that maybe a ghost guest will, like, join or whatever," Audrey said, flippantly, twisting her too-blonde hair around one manicured finger.

Her smile was practiced, vacant.

"You seriously asking questions right now? That's, like, kinda desperate."

Sarah let out a high, off-kilter laugh—sharp and too loud, like a tea kettle left screaming on the stove. "Yah, just chill. Don't overthink it, babe. We're here for, like, vibes."

Riya didn't respond, and her spine stiffened. She hated when people told her she "thought too much."

Haley never did—because thinking things through was how they survived. How they won.

Unlike the Malum sisters, who were starting to look less like real people and more like glitchy carnival dolls—faces stretched too tight over something hollow.

The air shifted.Audrey crouched, spreading a blanket like she was prepping a séance instead of a hangout. Her nails clicked against the fabric, sharp as a praying mantis's jaws.

"Cute, right?" she said with a deadpan grin. "Totally haunted picnic chic."

No one laughed.

Then Audrey dropped into a perfect butterfly stretch, calm as a cat in a sunbeam.

"Sit," she said sweetly, like a command disguised as an invitation.

Riya stepped forward, her voice flat. "Quick question," she said, tilting her head like a detective mid-interrogation. "Did you light those freaky candles before we showed up... or what?"

She pointed to the glowing pillars circling the blankets.

"Because they're really creepy," Riya muttered. "That wax? It's all thick and lumpy—like leftover taco grease. Or, worse, cursed slime someone dares you to touch."

Audrey's head snapped around so fast her hair tangled at the base of her skull like a knotted wig.

"Oh my gosh, chill," she said, waving it off. "Sarah and I, like, picked them up at some thrift store, O-kay? They're organic or whatever."

She wrapped a strand of hair around her finger, tight enough to cut off feeling—then smiled.

"Can't say you're wrong though," she drawled, eyes going glassy. "They might be made from... leftovers. You know, like the people who 'moved away' right after the block parties."

Riya's breath hitched. She'd heard the whispers—rumors at school that Audrey and Sarah's parties were invite-only. And afterward, people would just... vanish.

Move away. No notice, no goodbyes.

It had always felt off. But now? Now it felt deliberate. The disappearances. The stories. The candles.

Riya hesitated—then Haley tugged her down. Their knees touched the others'.

Audrey's eyes gleamed. "We're gathered to honor the spirits of Hallows' Eve. This story? Totally true. And it starts right here."

Sarah's voice cut the stillness. "There was once a queen whose powers were stolen. She vowed revenge."

The candle flames flared.

Audrey traced lazy circles in the mist. "The queen hexed these second-rate baby witches just to make sure they couldn't put the universe back together again."

She leaned in closer, her grin sharp as broken glass.

"And the curse?" she purred, tilting her head like a broken doll. "It can only be broken if one of them dies."

She rocked back and forth like she was easing into a trance—then shrieked.

"Because her cousin has to KILL HER!"

She giggled, a high, glittery sound like shattered sugar glass—but her eyes didn't laugh. They burned.

Riya jolted like she'd been slapped. She scrambled to her feet, voice cracking. "Wait—what did you just say? What?!"

The clearing spun sideways.

This wasn't just a spooky story circle. This was a trap. No—worse.

A broken hex gone completely wrong.

The candles and their pressed knees didn't make a cute little ring.

They made a shape.

A star. *An eight-pointed star.*

Haley's breath hitched. They'd done it. Completed the curse.

And set Hexima free.

"Ray—what did I do?!" Haley shrieked, panic bubbling up fast.

"I don't know! You're the one who thought it was a good idea to follow the sketchy sisters into the woods!"

"WELL, MAYBE DON'T LET ME MAKE DECISIONS NEXT TIME!" Haley snapped.

Then they heard it.

Low. Wet. Gnawing. Like flesh being chewed behind a wall.

Riya grabbed Haley's hand. "Tell me that's *not* what I think it is," she whispered.

But Haley couldn't. Because whatever it was... It was getting closer.

CHAPTER THIRTY-ONE

ONE DAY BEFORE HALLOWEEN

It began as a hiss—low, sharp—then split into a shriek, a chorus of snarls.

From the shadows, a dozen Shiverskins swarmed in—a single ripple of terror.

Eyes black as coal. Limbs bent wrong, joints snapping with insect precision. Mouths gaping too wide, teeth flashing in the candlelight.

Riya froze, every muscle locking like the air had turned to stone.

"Please tell me those are just, like... really committed Halloween costumes."

Haley didn't blink.

"If they are," she said, voice low, "they'd win every costume contest that's ever existed... and then eat the judges." One Shiverskin snapped its head toward them, neck popping like a broken hinge. Another dropped to all fours, claws raking the dirt in fast, fevered scrapes.

"RUN!" Riya shrieked.

Riya and Haley bolted into the woods.

The fog clawed at their knees. Branches whipped their faces. The earth seemed alive, trying to trip them with rising roots.

Behind them, Audrey's voice rang out—creepy and cold, like an ancient curse.

"You won't get far," the voice sneered. "Hexima's already on her way... and she's starving!"

A Shiverskin lunged. Its claws shredded Haley's jacket. She screamed, stumbling.

Riya turned and slapped it back with her full strength. "My Chemisource—" she panted. "Maybe I can summon Inky!"

She clenched her fists. Shut her eyes. Focused. Nothing.

"RAY!" Haley cried again, another Shiverskin barreling toward them.

"INKY—GET HERE. NOW!" Riya screamed.

CRACK.

The fog tore open like paper.

Inky shot through the sky like a dragonfly outrunning raindrops—smacking the Shiverskin square in the face.

It crumpled, releasing a sound somewhere between a wheeze and nails gargling down a drain.

The book ricocheted, spun with unnecessary flourish, and burst mid-air in a shower of golden light—cosmic confetti raining down.

Its pages snapped open, words writhing and glowing like they were desperate to break free.

The cousins didn't think. They jumped—straight into the light.

The world split with a sound like glass giving way—too fast, too hard—until up and down didn't matter, until their stomachs and souls felt equally untethered.

Then it came—her voice, echoing like it had crossed centuries just to find them:

"You're late."

A woman stood before them—radiant, as if the moon itself had chosen a human form.

CHAPTER THIRTY-TWO

ONE DAY BEFORE HALLOWEEN

Her skin shimmered—deep bronze kissed by sunlight. Tight black curls framed her face, each coil dusted with gold, as if they'd stolen the last light of dying stars.

She looked at the cousins as if awestruck, though her endless brown eyes—galaxies folded within them—had seen it all.

A white pantsuit wrapped her tall frame like woven stormfire. Above her hovered a single ring of brilliance, spun from star shavings and living flame, orbiting in slow, deliberate turns.

The hall hushed. Her very presence thrummed with power.

Queen Zion had arrived.

"Welcome to Sphalum." Her words dripped like molten gold, carrying the hush of a storm before it breaks. "The Lightwices. Heirs of the Fates... at last you stand where the heavens themselves have conspired to place you."

The cousins stood breathless, barely nodding their heads.

Zion stepped forward, her moonstone amulet swaying from a golden chain.

Inside it shimmered with impossible colors—cotton-candy pink, electric blue, deep-space white.

Scenes flashed within it: the past, the present... and something darker still. She studied them in silence, then gave a single solemn nod.

"You now understand what is at stake. You must go back. And you must not fail."

From the folds of her silken pocket, Zion drew out two glowing amulets.

"To you, Ms. Riya, I return your birthright," she said, placing the first around Riya's neck. The clamshell-sized white crystal pulsed with full-spectrum light.

"This amulet bestows upon you the gift of the Healux," Queen Zion said, her voice rich and steady. "With it, you hold the power to mend more than flesh—you may reach beyond the Veil and summon life itself. But be warned."

Her fingers grazed the stone, reverent and grave.

"Should your intentions stray toward vanity or personal gain, the onu you restore will return not whole... but corrupted, and irrevocably twisted."

Riya's stone flickered, dimmed, and for one breath... turned coal black.

Zion turned to Haley.

An amulet drifted down into Haley's hands, the silver chain coiling midair—untouched by gravity, as if even the laws of nature dared not interfere.

It shimmered like dragon scales dipped in molten bronze and midnight cocoa, catching light with every breath she took.

Queen Zion's gaze never wavered.

"And to you, Ms. Haley, the power of Zeno. You may reverse time and rewrite the universe. Yet if used selfishly, you will answer to the Door of Bones."

Haley's breath hitched. Her knees buckled, but she stood her ground.

Zion's voice deepened, echoing through the shimmering hall.

"You have summoned *The Book of Fates*." Her words carried the hush of ancient halls, as though the universe itself leaned in to listen. "That means you are ready to stand among the Fates. But hear me well—Queen Hexima's rotten spirit now prowls... and what has been set free will not be bound again."

Haley's voice wavered. "So... what can we do now?"

"You return to the moment before you opened the door," Zion said smoothly. "And rewrite history in your favor."

Riya stepped forward. "If we go back... will we remember this?"

Zion inclined her head, the motion slow and deliberate. "You will. No one else will. That is both your gift... and your burden. But remember this—" her voice dropped—"something dark lurks in the underbelly of the Lightwice home. I cannot remove it. Only you can summon its end."

"Hold tight," Zion said. "This journey will not be gentle."

The air cracked. Light tore through the space. Inky shot down from the sky, pages flapping like frantic wings.

"Think of your questions," Zion called. "The universe is listening."

Riya clutched her amulet. Haley shut her eyes.

Together, they jumped—

—just as the light behind them shattered like glass.

Then—

WHUMP.

They crash-landed in a heap of vintage sweaters and mismatched pillows—smack in the middle of Haley's attic, like a sleepover gone sideways.

The crooked lamp waited in the corner, Halloween decorations teetered on the table's edge, and the terrarium faintly hummed—alive with odd-looking toads.

It all looked... normal.

Too normal.

"Did it work?" Riya whispered, rubbing her elbow.

Ding-dong.

The doorbell rang.

Haley turned slowly, her breath catching in her throat. "Is that...?"

Three heavy knocks followed.

Bang. Bang. *BANG.*

The cousins froze.

This was it.

A branch between two futures.

Riya let go of the ladder, wood clacking into place behind them, knowing full well—the end of everything was only the beginning.

CHAPTER THIRTY-THREE

ONE DAY BEFORE HALLOWEEN

The cousins tiptoed downstairs, feet barely grazing the steps—they couldn't risk Audrey or Sarah hearing them, not after what they'd seen, not after what they knew.

Time travel had rules, right? Unwritten, terrifying rules.

Riya felt like a polar bear dropped in the middle of a desert—hot, confused, and definitely about to die.

"Hales..." she whispered, stretching the word like taffy. "What if going back was a total mistake? Like, even breathing wrong could mess up everything."

"I seriously doubt my sighs are gonna wreck the universe," Haley muttered, arms crossed.

"I've seen enough time travel movies to know it totally could!" Riya hissed. "One wrong move and—boom—apocalypse."

Haley sighed. "Okay, fine. We try to do everything the same. Except this time," she paused, staring at the front door like it might bite, "we keep that thing shut."

Riya flailed her arms. "Ugh! Too late! We already messed up—we didn't talk before opening the door last time!"

The middle stair groaned like a ghost waking up. They both froze.

Beneath it lay a hidden stash: weapons of majick, sharp and deadly, humming with stored power. Enough to fry anything undead, enchanted, or worse.

"Hey, Ray," Haley whispered, a crooked smile curling up. "Should we...

grab something? Maybe the fika? That bow and arrow thing that turns monsters into sparkles?"

Riya chewed her lip. "Part of me wants to, like, turn them into glittery gut soup...but no. We stick to the plan. No weapons."

Haley nodded, but her voice cracked. "Right. No weapons."

SLAM. WHAM. BANG!

The door rattled. The frame buzzed like a bug zapper on overdrive. Riya's heart triple-bounced against her ribs.

Together, they edged toward the skinny window beside the door—just wide enough for a peek... or a very bad mistake.

Haley leaned in.

"I don't see anyone. Think they finally—"

WHAM.

A grotesque hand smacked the glass. Purple. Rotting. Glistening like it had been dipped in motor oil and then shoved into a blender.

Two sickly, half-rotted figures staggered into view—limbs jerking like puppets on tangled strings, eyes clouded with something not entirely dead.

Haley gasped. "Audrey? Sarah?! What the actual—?"

Riya dove for cover. "Ohmygodohmygod—they're undead!"

Audrey and Sarah didn't move. They just stood there...grinning.

Audrey tilted her head, her lip dangling by a thread like wet paper. "Sarah and I were thinking of heading into the woods. Swap scary stories, stir up some spooky vibes. You in?"

"Wanna join?" Sarah chimed in, her voice syrupy-sweet. A clump of her corn-husk-blonde hair slid from her scalp and hit the welcome mat with a soft *plop*.

She didn't even blink.

Riya gagged. "Gross, ew. Halloween came early, or Zion seriously glitched."

A piece of Sarah's forehead peeled off like a slice of deli meat.

"EW," Riya groaned, slapping a hand over her mouth. "They're LITERALLY falling apart. That's not makeup!"

The dead were no longer resting.

Haley reached for Riya's wrist, ready to drag her back upstairs—but Audrey took a slow, jerky step forward.

"Haley," Audrey rasped, her voice like gravel dragged across a chalkboard. *"Invite us in."*

Her cheek slipped off and slapped against the porch with a wet *slap*.

Riya dry-heaved. "I think I'm gonna puke."

The undead sisters knocked again—once, twice, three times—then turned without a word.

Their pink high heels clacked down the steps like broken metronomes, tottering into the fog and vanishing between the trees.

Silence settled back over the room like a held breath.

Riya slid down the wall, heart racing. "Um... d-do you think we just... turned them into zombies or something?"

Haley didn't answer at first. She was still staring at the fog.

Finally, she whispered, "I don't know."

Then she spun on her heel, bolting for the attic.

"Hales?" Riya called, scrambling after her. "Where are you going?"

Haley didn't stop—she was already halfway up the attic ladder.

"We need answers," she said. "Now."

She vanished into the loft.

Riya hesitated for a breath... then followed her.

Upstairs, Inky was open.

And it was already writing.

CHAPTER THIRTY-FOUR

ONE DAY BEFORE HALLOWEEN

Riya and Haley's breathing came fast—shaky, shallow, like they were trying to inhale answers that didn't exist.

"Um, please—please—tell us why Audrey and Sarah looked like melting Barbies left on a dashboard in July?" Riya groaned, throwing her hands up like she was surrendering to some magical traffic cop.

Inky didn't hesitate. Words scrawled across the parchment—hurried, bare, no flourish—just a single question.

What boon did you ask the cosmos when you returned from Queen Zion's?

"I asked how I could always see the truth," Riya said, puffing up slightly.
"Same here!" Haley added. "That's what I asked, too."
Inky's pages rustled like dry leaves.

Then I did nothing. You asked to see the truth.
Audrey and Sarah Malum come from a long line of Succubus Otherkin. Not vampires—worse. They do not drink blood. They drain—onus.
Queen Hexima planted them in your path to keep you weak. They've been feeding on your majick since the day you were born.

"So we've been, like... their magical juice boxes this whole time?" Riya whispered, hugging her knees. "I guess we're lucky they didn't slap straws in our necks and call it brunch," she muttered.

Haley let out a dry laugh. "Yeah. Soul smoothies—and with extra Lightwice."

Inky fluttered a page as if sighing dramatically.

Had you invited them in, they would have taken everything—your majick, your amulets, even your onus.

And I would not have been able to stop them.

You asked to see the truth. Now that you know it... your gloaming must begin.

Without delay.

Riya rocked on her heels, eyes fixed on the floor. "I don't know if I can do this. Feels like there's always gonna be someone—or something—coming for us. What's the point?"

Haley pushed Inky away gently. "Because if we don't fight back, they'll keep taking—first from us, then our family... then the world. We have to fight."

"Yeah, easy for you to say. You've got a power that could destroy galaxies. I've got... healing?"

Haley reached across and grabbed her hand. "You've got me."

Inky snapped to a new page, ink flaring across the parchment in wild, urgent strokes.

You were sent back in time—which means time is now your weapon... or your curse. That shift altered the Fates—your Fates.

Whether it brings salvation or destruction... only time will tell.

The clock is ticking. Prepare yourselves.

Even if one of you must die...

CHAPTER THIRTY-FIVE

ONE DAY BEFORE HALLOWEEN

The first time Riya heard one of them had to die, a talking book spelled it out.

The second time was in the woods—with the Malum sisters grinning like corpses.

Somehow, that wasn't even the weirdest part. What truly rattled her? She was starting to believe it.

Instantly, the book sprang to life, scribbling across the page with fierce determination.

The following steps are not optional. Follow them exactly. Review them carefully—your future, and the Fates, depend on it.

Step One: Enroll at Aetherion Academy and complete your gloaming.

Step Two: Haley must defeat the Shadow Gloze, guardian of the Shadow Veil, by striking the soft spot behind its right ear with her Athame.

Step Three: Slice your palms, press them together, and chant the Light Oath:

> *By blood we bind,*
> *With light we shine,*
> *Our Fates forever intertwined.*

Step Four: Call the Light Realms with the Unity Oath:

> *By blood and bond, by pain and power,*
> *We vow beneath this sacred hour—*
> *To guard the light, to fight the dark,*
> *To leave no soul without a spark.*
> *Let shadow know our names with fear,*
> *Let majick mark us ever near.*

Step Five: Travel to Dahmorte and defeat Queen Hexima's Maldrop army.
If victory is yours, the Charmwic Ball will rise in splendor—your family
gathered, the Veils restored.

Riya's jaw dropped. "Wait—Haley *actually* has to fight that beak-handed monster from our kitchen? The one that smelled like a diaper full of despair?"

Jabbing a finger into Inky's spine, she snapped, "Plan? More like a mythic to-do list with 'violent death' scribbled in the margins."

Haley exhaled slowly. "Yeah. But at least it ends with a dance."

Riya snorted. "Great. Guess I'd better start picking out my funeral playlist."

Inky wrote ominously.

Your greatest trial—and your gloaming—draws near.
Waste not the hour. Steel yourselves.

Haley's phone buzzed beneath her. A text from Raven:

Hey honey, what would you n Ray like 4 food 2nite?

Haley's face drained. "Ugh! It's three! They actually closed the shop early—they'll be home any minute!"

"Stall them!" Riya shouted, bolting upright.

Haley typed furiously:

Dinner? 2nite? That pasta place far from home. 2 red sauce plates, combos.
Please? Thx, Mom! XO!

"Okay. So that buys us, what—an hour? We need to figure out this gloaming now. Because tomorrow... I have to, like, kill a Gloze."

"Wait—what did you just say?" Riya gawked. "You sound way too chill about stabbing something."

"Just trying not to lose it," Haley muttered, biting her lip.

Riya flicked Inky's pages, the word *GLOAMING* shimmering like a party invite—but instead of cake and candles, it promised blood, bones, and something deadly.

She shot up from the bed and made a beeline for the door—

—But Haley grabbed her arm.

"Please, Ray! We have to do this before our parents get home!"

"Fine," Riya huffed. "But after this, we're definitely reviewing Inky's psycho game plan."

She smacked the book, as if it were an old TV.

Nothing. No writing. No flipping. Not even a flutter.

Silence.

Then came a knock—at the window.

CHAPTER THIRTY-SIX

ONE DAY BEFORE HALLOWEEN

A tiny broom—no bigger than a toddler's hand—wobbled outside the window, knocking like a sparrow on a mission.

Haley scrambled over. "Is that—? A flying toothbrush?"

Riya squinted. "I think it's a besom," she said, puffing up with pride in her growing magical vocab. "The magical broom thingy."

"Well, tell your fancy broom to chill," Haley muttered.

Riya threw open the window.

The little bristle brush zipped inside like it owned the place—darting left, juking right—then spun midair with the smug attitude of a cat knocking something off a shelf.

"But... why? And why my room? Or even this dimension?" Haley asked, arms crossed.

The besom hovered—judgy—then bopped her lightly on the forehead, like *Don't question the process, ash.*

Riya took a quick step back. "Nope. That's enough possessed cleaning supplies for one day."

The broom shot upward, smacked the ceiling fan with a *clank*, ricocheted off the wall, twirled like a drunken bat, and belly-flopped between them in a puff of glittery smoke.

Haley blinked. "Are those—?"

"Don't say it," Riya warned, snatching one out of the air. "Because if we just got invited to a magical death ball or something, I swear I'm setting something on fire."

Haley picked up the second ticket. It shimmered with embossed letters that shifted when tilted.

You have been cordially accepted into the Aetherion Academy.
Attendance is mandatory.

They exchanged a look.

"I mean... *mandatory* is a strong word," Riya muttered, clutching her ticket like it might bite her.

"But you know we're going," Haley sighed. "Right?"

Riya groaned. "Fine. But I'm wearing sneakers. I draw the line at toe blisters."

Riya snatched the tickets up, shook off more glitter, and read:

Your ride will be arriving shortly.

She rushed to the window. "Nope. This is a terrible idea!"

A flying machine hovered outside, shaped like a giant garbage sculpture. All gears, gadgets, and glitter glue.

Riya squinted. "Is that... a doll head stuck on a fork antenna?"

A low humming started. It rose to a whirlwind that flipped the room upside-down.

Lamps on the ceiling. Fans on the floor. Homework tornado.

They dove under the covers just as a pair of bright yellow eyes popped into view, framed by two pointy bat ears.

A cat-faced pilot with cracked leather goggles and a voice like static yelled through the window, "Jump in, ladies! Name's Tayka—I'm your ride to Aetherion Academy! And we're officially late!"

Behind her, the sky split open with a thunderclap that didn't sound like weather.

Haley peeked over the blanket. "Uh... what happens if we don't go with you?" she shouted over the rumble of the flying death trap.

Tayka's cat-eyes narrowed behind her goggles. "Then the Gloze eats your onus, Hexima conquers the Fates, and the universe ends in eternal darkness. So, ya know... no pressure!"

Steam hissed through a pipe, then—*pop*—sparks burst into the air.

Riya yelped. "We're gonna die before the gloaming even starts!"

"Ten seconds!" Tayka barked. "Doors close on destiny!"

Below them, the floorboards moaned. The air turned cold.

Something whispered their Fates. Something old. Something wise.

174

The cousins locked eyes—and jumped.

CHAPTER THIRTY-SEVEN

One Day Before Halloween

Tayka's bat ears twitched as she tapped a rhythm on the wheel with her spider-monkey fingers.

"Cargo's aboard. Destination: Aetherion Academy. Over and out," she crackled into her headset.

She glanced back. "Don't worry 'bout your room, sugar cakes. It'll be good as new when y'all get back."

The flying machine lurched forward, slicing through bare branches and skimming treetops. Main Street blurred beneath them—roofs streaked by like candy-colored smudges.

"Can anyone see us in this flying... toaster?" Riya asked, squinting at the town below.

"Nope. We're invisible, darlin'," Tayka said with a grin. "Folks might feel a breeze, but they won't see a thing. Oh, and she's not a toaster. This is a Fooka. Her name's Maggie—and she runs on moondust."

"Yeah," Riya muttered. "Of course, the universe runs on a moondust machine named Maggie."

The engine purred louder as they sped toward a sky-high waterfall of icy mist.

"Uh... what's that?" Riya asked, pointing.

Tayka didn't answer—just hit the throttle.

"WAIT—SLOW DOWN!" Riya shrieked.

Too late.

Maggie flipped sideways and cut through the barrier. It hissed like dry ice in boiling water, searing the air as ghostly blue-white flames licked its edges.

Riya's throat tensed, ready to unleash a baby-goat scream—

—but Tayka glanced back with an easy smile.

"That was Ice Fire. It protects the Veils," she said, calm as if she were naming a paint color. "You can't pass through without your amulets. Without 'em? You'd be toast. Like... actual, bread-in-a-toaster toast."

She held up her pink amulet.

Riya and Haley instinctively gripped theirs tighter, both silently realizing they were wildly underqualified for this journey.

The world beyond looked torn from a dream—or the aftermath of a surreal explosion.

The ground shimmered like glitter-frosted cupcakes. Curvy homes with twisty, corkscrew roofs leaned toward one another as if whispering secrets.

From each rounded chimney drifted slow, drowsy pillows of smoke—lavender, mint, and rose-scented—that curled into lazy shapes before dissolving.

Tiny, winged postboxes zipped between doors, trailing ribbons of parchment.

A cluster of teacups floated across a balcony rail, clinking softly like gossiping neighbors.

Somewhere, a bell chimed, and the whole place seemed to exhale.

Above them, twin suns poured molten gold across the streets, their light catching on stained-glass windows that winked in every color imaginable.

Bug-winged fairies zipped past, goggles perched on their tiny noses.

"They're from the Fiff," Tayka said, waving. "Basically majickal text messages."

Snowflakes drifted down, catching gold light from a winding stream.

Tayka pointed ahead.

"Here in Sphalum, time runs a day and a season ahead—winter morning for us, but in your Veil it's still autumn, halfway through lunch."

The Maggie tilted downward.

A freezing gust slapped the cousins' cheeks as Tayka tossed them puffy jackets.

"These'll keep ya warm. Now—see that little red door? Knock once. Hand the gatekeeper your tickets. And if you need me?"

She flashed a grin, goggles winking gold.

"Just holler 'Tayka,' and I'll come flyin'—no matter where in the skies I am."

CHAPTER THIRTY-EIGHT

One Day Before Halloween

Bundled up, the cousins trekked through the glittering snow, their breath fogging the air like dragon smoke.

Lanterns shaped like floating snowflakes drifted overhead, glowing with trapped starlight.

Signs swung from candy-cane-striped poles, advertising things like Invisible Ice Cream, Glow-Up Goblets, and Hair That Screams™.

Riya accidentally stepped on something squishy.

"Hey! Watch it!" barked a brick that sprouted legs and stormed off, grumbling in a gravelly accent.

"Was that a... talking pebble?" Riya blinked.

"Yup," Haley said. "Super stony welcome."

The shops lining the winding cobblestone path were wild—self-stirring spoons danced in teacups, pet toads let out high-pitched banshee screams, and soda bottles floated mid-air, changing flavors with your mood.

A sentient scarf floated by and tried to wrap around Riya's neck. She swatted it away.

But the cheerful chaos was oddly quiet. Doors slammed at their approach. Curtains were drawn. Even the wind seemed to hush around them.

"Why is everyone acting like we're the problem?" Riya muttered.

"Don't know... We've got amulets," Haley said. "Pretty sure that means we belong here."

A teacup-sized troll with a single glowing eye waddled over and kicked Riya in the shin. Hard.

"OW! What is my magical karma today?!" she snapped.

Finally, they reached a rounded red door nestled between two mushroom-shaped cottages.

It opened with a rusty creak, revealing a blue-chested ogre nearly the size of a refrigerator.

She loomed in silence.

"Yes," she hissed, arms folded like stone pillars.

Riya handed over the tickets. The ogre sniffed them once, then nodded.

"You shall pass." She smiled—a mouth full of jagged pearls.

The Veil shimmered shut with a soft *shhhpt*.

Inside, the air buzzed like static.

Then—*ZAP!*

A bolt of magical lightning cracked through the room, slamming into Haley's shoulder.

"OW! What the actual—?!" Haley clutched her arm, the spot still crackling. "Great. Guess my magical karma's having a meltdown too."

A tall, regal woman approached, wrapped in a velvet robe that shimmered between storm blue and tree-bark brown.

Her skin gleamed like polished mahogany, her eyes the color of dark sap—unreadable and steady.

She regarded them as if they were unexpected guests at a very exclusive party.

"Ms. Riya. Ms. Haley," she said, her voice smooth and unbothered. "How lovely of you to crash in."

Her tone was deep, melodic—almost too calm for everything they'd just been through.

"I am Ms. Treewith," she added, as if that explained everything. "We are the Rede."

Two more figures appeared in a swirl of cloaks—Ms. Haute, with her jewel-studded satchel of herbs, and Mr. Seacoal, dripping mist as if he'd just emerged from a wave.

The cousins gasped in unison.

"Oh my gosh—it's you!" Riya blurted, eyes wide.

"You're exactly like the book described," Haley added, stepping forward like she was meeting a myth.

Ms. Haute's smile bloomed—warm, practiced, and just perfect.

"And you're just what we expected—bright, sharp, and full of promise."

A shadow passed between them.

Ms. Treewith's expression soured. "Enough cooing. Follow me."

She spun around, the sharp click of her pointed heels echoing like flint against steel.

Ms. Haute leaned in with a conspiratorial whisper. "Don't mind her. She hasn't had breakfast yet."

"I heard that," Ms. Treewith barked, her voice clipped, heels stabbing the floor as she led them deeper inside.

They walked through a corridor of twisting silver vines and bookshelves that rearranged themselves at will.

Strange paintings followed their every move—one of a melting moon, another of a crying sun.

"Why was everyone so cold to us?" Haley asked, glancing back at a self-sweeping broom that was glaring at her.

Ms. Haute sighed. "They're afraid. If you fail to restore the Fates... everything ends."

Riya gulped, her voice barely a whisper. "That ogre... the one who let us in. What was she?"

Ms. Haute's warm blue eyes dimmed, sorrow pooling in their depths.

"Her name is Zea," she said softly. "One of the last Light Glozes—creatures born of balance and ancient majick. Each Gloze is soul-bound to a partner. Zea's mate, Rea, was stolen from her centuries ago... by Queen Hexima."

Riya's brows knit. "Stolen how?"

"Rea was corrupted," Ms. Haute said softly. "Condemned to guard the Shadow Veil... a gatekeeper of evil for all eternity."

Riya blinked, horrified. "And Zea still let us in? Even though Haley's about to go full slayer on her undead girlfriend?"

"She still remembers their love," Ms. Haute said, voice cracking. "But she knows what must be done."

Riya didn't miss a beat. Her voice trembled.

"So... just making sure I'm tracking," Riya whispered, her voice thin and disbelieving. "Haley has to *kill* someone's actual soulmate?"

Saying it out loud made it land harder, like the truth had finally shown up and taken a seat.

Ms. Haute's silence said everything.

Haley's breath hitched.

"Why... me?" she asked, barely audible.

Ms. Treewith answered coldly from ahead. "Because no one else can."

Haley flinched, slow, shaky, like she could just brush the truth off her sleeve.

"Well, it can't be worse than that zap I got walking in and—"

Ms. Treewith's heels struck the stone, spinning her in a tight whirl.

"You," she hissed, her voice cutting through the room like splitting firewood, "astral projected to Everbind."

She leveled a long finger at Haley, scolding like a child.

"And in doing so..." Ms. Treewith's eyes burned—ancient, furious—"you dragged Hexima's spirit and an Elemental back with you. That zap wasn't random. It was the Veil's answer to your recklessness."

Haley stumbled over her words. "I... I didn't mean to—"

Ms. Treewith raised a paper-thin hand, silencing her like a slammed book.

"No one means to open the door to corruption," she said coolly. "But once it's open... it doesn't close quietly."

The room felt colder.

Riya shifted beside Haley, her fingers curling into fists.

"She was trying to help our moms," Riya snapped. "She didn't know Hexima would hitch a ride back!"

Ms. Treewith's gaze settled on Riya. "The purity of ones intent does not lessen the weight of a deed."

Her eyes blazed, the air around her sparking with the kind of fury that made candles flicker without flame.

"So, yes," she hissed, stepping closer, her shadow spilling across the floor like a warning. "Your gloaming will be excruciating."

The Rede raised their hands.

Their chant began—low and ancient. Pain surged through Riya and Haley like fire ants under their skin—hot, endless, alive.

Haley dropped first. Her lips blued. Her limbs twitched.

"STOP! NOW!" Riya shouted, dragging herself toward her cousin—

But her legs gave out.

She crumpled beside Haley, their fingers brushing like the last flicker of a dying fire.

Riya's voice was a ghost of a breath.

"I'm sorry..."

And then—

The world snapped shut. Darkness swallowed everything.

CHAPTER THIRTY-NINE

One Day Before Halloween

The dark wasn't empty. It erased—like the world scribbled out of existence.

No stars to steer by, no breath to anchor the living.

It wrapped around Riya like a weighted shroud stitched from death's hand, pressing on her chest until thought, memory, and meaning curled like paper in an open flame.

She couldn't move. Couldn't scream. Couldn't *be*.

And then—

A whisper. A flicker—A memory.

Warmth on her skin. Sunlight slanting through a window.

Sticky fingers. Bare feet. A summer afternoon. The scent of sunscreen and burnt toast.

Haley's laugh—high, real—bounced off the cul-de-sac pavement as she chased her through the grass, arms flailing, eyes bright.

The memory blazed, more vivid than fear.

Riya clung to it.

Because if this darkness wanted to swallow her whole—It would have to earn her.

Then came sound. Wind rushing past her ears. A thousand whispers, circling like leaves in a storm. All saying the same thing.

"Riya... Riya... Riya..."

She gasped—then bolted upright. Air. Real air.

The silver-lit room of Aetherion Academy unfolded around her like a dream trying to remember itself.

The chanting had stopped.

The Rede were gone.

But Haley—

Her cousin lay crumpled beside her.

"Haley!" Riya gasped, scrambling to her knees.

She grabbed her shoulders and shook her gently. Pressed her forehead to Haley's chest.

Silence. No breath. No beat.

Tears threatened—but didn't fall. This wasn't grief. Not yet. This was terror. Raw, blinding panic—A scream sealed behind her ribs, pounding to get out.

Her fingers brushed the cold amulet at her throat. It pulsed. Once. Strong.

Riya's breath caught. She gripped it hard.

Zion's voice echoed in her head: *You are a Healux.*

She shut her eyes. Blocked out the chaos. The room. The way the air still tasted like burnt herbs and endings.

She focused instead on the rhythm of her heartbeat. The inhale. The exhale.

With trembling fingers, Riya reached out and placed her hand over Haley's chest.

Nothing.

No rise. No fall. No warmth. Only more stillness.

"Please," she whispered, her voice cracking open like a broken wish. "I can't do this without you."

Something tightened in her chest—defiance. Like her soul was refusing to surrender.

The amulet sparked—deep black at first, like the void had blinked. Then gold.

Heat surged through Riya's veins like liquid hope.

And then—

The air rippled. The floor beneath her cracked with a thunderous groan. The amulet lifted from her chest, weightless, crowned in light.

And from her fingertips, the light poured—spooling down into Haley's heart like melted jelly.

And just before the world exploded again—Riya swore she heard a heartbeat that wasn't her own.

Haley jerked. Coughed. Gasped.

Her eyes fluttered open.

"Ray?" she rasped.

Riya let out a choked laugh and threw her arms around Haley, squeezing her like a life raft.

"Okay—I'm alive, not a pancake," Haley wheezed. "Ease up, or I might not stay that way."

Riya pulled back, her cheeks streaked with tears. "You're okay," she whispered, voice shaking. "I thought I lost you."

Haley blinked up at her, disoriented. "What... what just happened?"

"Gloaming," Riya said. "Apparently... with a side of dying."

Haley closed her eyes. "It felt like falling forever."

She touched her amulet. It shimmered faintly, like it remembered.

"Well... that was the worst final exam ever. Nearly died, no study guide, and I'm pretty sure I failed the part where you're supposed to stay conscious."

They stood slowly, legs trembling, everything inside them different now.

"Do you feel... weird?" Riya asked.

Haley nodded. "Like someone installed Wi-Fi in my soul."

Riya blinked. "I feel like I could hug a tree and make it bloom."

They exchanged a look—equal parts terrified and awestruck.

"And," Riya muttered, eyes wide, "the back of my neck is on fire."

"Me too," Haley croaked. She winced. "Hey... can you look?"

Riya gently parted Haley's frizzed curls—and gasped. "Um. You've got... your mom's weird scar thing."

"WHAT?!" Haley screeched. She slapped a hand over the burning spot. "Oh no-no-no—let me check you."

Haley spun Riya around, lifted her hair, and froze.

"You've got one too," she whispered.

Riya clutched her curls like emotional-support noodles. "Are you telling me we survived a cursed ogre in our kitchen, a murder-knife talent show, and time-bending magic—just to get branded?"

Haley blinked. "Yup."

"Oh, cool. Totally normal."

Riya threw up her hands and added. "Nothing says personal growth like matching trauma scars from the universe."

Rushed footsteps echoed.

Ms. Treewith appeared in the doorway, her expression unreadable.

"You survived. Let's hope it was worth it."

Riya raised an eyebrow. "No coffee? Bagels? Just trauma and sarcasm?"

Ms. Treewith didn't smile. "The Fates expect you before sunset tomorrow. Your first task awaits."

She turned without another word and disappeared into the shadows.

Riya and Haley stood in silence. They laced fingers, turned—and found

Inky hovering at their feet, flapping its pages like it was about to take flight.

"No, Tayka? No, Maggie?" Riya asked, hopefully.

Inky flipped open to a glowing page.

Riya groaned. "Guess not." She crossed her arms. "I was starting to like that rattling death-trap."

A whoosh of light swallowed them whole—the world tilted, spun—then hit with a bone-deep *thud*.

They crash-landed in a heap of tangled blankets and glittery smoke, smack in the middle of Haley's bedroom.

Outside, car doors slammed.

"Oh no," Riya whispered.

The front door creaked open.

"Girls? We got pasta!" Raven called—voice light, too cheerful. Suspiciously cheerful.

Haley bolted upright, eyes wide. "Pasta. Oh my stars. Real food."

Riya stared at her. "How can you think about food after what we just went through?"

"Why aren't you?" Haley hissed, clutching her stomach like it might collapse. "Do you think they got garlic knots? Please tell me they got garlic knots."

But the moment shattered into panic.

They scrambled—tossing blankets, smoothing hair, wiping tears, pretending they hadn't just been to the edge of death and back. Their amulets vanished under hoodies.

Inky dove under a pillow like it was playing dead.

Footsteps echoed up the stairs.

"Act normal!" Riya whisper-screeched, brown eyes wide and wild. "Wait—what's normal, anyway?!"

Too late.

A shadow fell across the hallway. The doorknob turned.

And all they could smell... was garlic.

Celeste and Raven walked in, looking half-asleep and half-overcaffeinated, muttering about weird customers, overdue orders, and how the moon "felt off again."

Their arms were full of takeout and stress. Their energy was peak mom-chaos meets lunar suspicion.

The cousins tried to act casual over red-sauce pasta and way too much garlic—despite looking like they'd just been launched through a tornado of stars, secrets, and emotional trauma.

Riya's curls were still tangled with attic dust and maybe a leaf from another dimension. Haley's shirt was on inside out.

Raven and Celeste, too spellbound and sleep-deprived to notice much, didn't even blink.

"You two look... focused," Raven said.

"Yep," Riya said through a bite. "Studied so hard I saw time bend."

"Same," Haley added solemnly. "Definitely learned... stuff."

Riya and Haley's eyes screamed cosmic battle, but their mouths said, *'Mmm, carbs.' Thanks, Mom!*

Their moms nodded, satisfied, and wandered off with wine glasses in hand—zero suspicion, complete trust.

The cousins collapsed, chewing like it was the only thing tethering their souls to Earth.

Because honestly? It might've been.

The empty takeout boxes were shuffled to the hallway like room service at a magical hotel. That was as far as they were willing to walk.

"Do you think we'll ever be normal again?" Riya whispered.

Haley pulled the blankets to her chin. "We never were."

They drifted off to the soft hum of Inky's closed-eye breath.

Tomorrow wouldn't just bring more magic—it would bring the *reckoning.*

Bloodlines would clash. The Fates would splinter.

And one of them might have to kill something other than the Gloze.

191

CHAPTER FORTY

HALLOWEEN

Riya was already sitting up in bed before the sun had a chance to cut through the fog curling at the windows.

Morning hadn't fully arrived—

But the world was awake enough to feel heavy. Sadness didn't pour in all at once—it sifted down slow, like dust from a crumbling ceiling.

Quiet. Suffocating.

Riya's chest felt tight. Not from fear. Not even from exhaustion. Just... grief.

A kind she didn't have words for yet.

That same, horrible voice whispered in her head: *What if you fail? What if Haley dies?* Her stomach churned.

Beside her, Haley was still asleep—curled like a comma—one arm flung across the blanket like she'd tried to anchor herself to something in her dreams.

Riya didn't wake her. She just sat there in the half-light, staring into the mist, and wondering if the world would ever feel right again.

And deep in the folds of too many quilts, Inky's pages rustled—quietly at first, like a sigh between thoughts. Like it already knew.

"Today's the day," Riya whispered, her voice brushing the edge of panic.

Haley groaned from beneath the covers.

The blankets clung to her like armor, thick and warm and unwilling to let go.

She wasn't ready to face the day—especially not *this* day. Not the morning she was supposed to slay a nightmare.

She sat up slowly, her legs heavy with dread, breath uneven. "Ray... I don't know if I can do it. Like... actually stab that thing."

Her voice cracked on the word *thing*, as if speaking it aloud might summon it—might make it real.

Inky rustled. A fresh page inked itself in deliberate, looping script.

Good morning, my Gloze slayer!
Please pick up the Athame and focus on it.

Haley winced. "Yeah," she yawned, rubbing her eyes. "Not helping."

Grumbling, Haley picked it up.

Instantly, a jolt shot up Haley's arm. She tried to drop the Athame—but her hand wouldn't budge.

Then—

Snap. Crack. POP.

A vision slammed into her skull.

The cave. The Gloze. It lunged—beaks slicing air—then Riya's neck. Blood sprayed the stone like paint from a shattered bucket.

Haley snapped upright with a blink, breath caught in her throat.

"I saw it," she rasped. "It—Ray, it killed you."

Riya froze. "Wait, what? Killed who? Like... you had a vision?!"

Inky's pages fluttered violently, as if caught in an invisible wind.

Haley—your vision was not a warning. It was a promise.
Hesitate, and you both fall.
Dahmorte does not wait. It feeds.
Linger too long, and it will claim you, onu first.
Riya—only you can pull Haley back. Do it fast. Do it before the Shadow learns her name.

Riya's voice cracked. "Wait—we could die? Like, actually die? Not metaphorically, not 'oops, cosmic fail'—real dead?"

Inky didn't move. Didn't flip. Just let the truth hang there, heavy and final.

Her chest tightened. Fingers curled into fists.

"You're saying after all this—the gloaming, the so-called immortality-maker—we're still killable?"

She threw back the covers in a huff. Her curls frizzed and snapped like live

194

wires.

"We're just bait with amulets. Like, death-by-a-nightmare-chicken-with-knife-hands!"

She spun on Inky, eyes blazing.

"I thought we were chosen. Destined. Protected."

Yes. You are both immortal, but not to Queen Hexima's Gloze.
Not to Queen Hexima herself.
That kind of seething, ancient evil does not just end lives—It ends worlds.
Even I cannot shield you from the Shadow born with the raw talent to make
galaxies and onus suffer.

Haley's voice came soft, but strong. "I need you, Ray. I can't do this alone."

Riya swallowed hard, blinking fast.

Her insides felt like they were shrinking. "You won't... if we die," she murmured, knees wobbling, lungs two sizes too small.

Her gaze dropped to the Athame glinting in Haley's grip.

"If I die before high school graduation," she muttered, "I'm haunting everyone."

Haley didn't answer. She scribbled a note to their parents:

Dear Mom and Dad,
We love you. Riya and I have to go—don't freak.
If we don't make it back... find the Book of Fates. It'll tell you why.
Love always,
Haley & Riya

Then—

Snap.

The air turned cold. Not winter-cold—dead-cold.

A shiver rolled down Riya's spine as the temperature dropped, fast and unnatural. Fog slithered beneath the door, curling around their ankles like it had claws.

Before either of them could move—

WHOOSH.

The world snapped sideways. Riya barely caught Haley's hand before the room evaporated.

Last time Inky dragged them through its pages, it had felt like being stretched thin and slammed back together in the blink of an eye.

195

But this time—time itself seemed to vanish.

Because they hit the ground—hard—inside the Gloze's cave.

Then—it hit them instantly. The stench.

Mold, skunk, and something worse—burnt hair and decay, like the memory of something that had once been alive and was very much not anymore.

The ground pulsed beneath their feet, slick and oozing like it was breathing through rot. Black vines hung from the ceiling like the cave had grown hair—slimy, stringy hair.

Riya gagged.

"This place is way worse than I remember," she whispered, covering her nose. "It's straight-up nightmare fuel! Like if a haunted house barfed on a sewer and lit it on fire."

Haley didn't answer.

She was staring ahead. Frozen.

Something had moved.

And it wasn't the fog.

CHAPTER FORTY-ONE

HALLOWEEN

Haley clutched the Athame tightly. It buzzed in her palm.

"Where is it?" She whispered.

As if summoned—a *thud* echoed—the curse with beaked hands had appeared.

The Gloze wasn't just a monster—it was walking doom.

Its hulking body twisted with joints that cracked sideways, too many elbows bending the wrong way. Its skin oozed a dark sheen—half oil, half rotted velvet—slick and wet, like something dredged from a tar pit.

Its face was a boar's parody, hollow sockets burning dull crimson, rows of needle-teeth clicking like a clock counting down.

But the six wildly whipping hands—wicked, talon-fused beaks—made anything the cousins had ever seen in a horror movie look like a cartoon. They didn't just slice—they harvested.

And then—it lunged.

Haley's eyes ignited, lit from within by the Zeno power—and suddenly, she saw everything. She shoved Riya aside, leapt, flipped, landed hard—then slashed.

Slush.

Flesh, shadow—didn't matter. It tore just the same. Tar sprayed the walls.

The Gloze roared.

Riya stepped forward, heart hammering. "HEY! Over here, you moldy chicken nugget!" she shouted, voice bouncing off the cave walls.

The Gloze turned, all beaks and shadow.

But Haley was already behind it—silent, steady—Athame in hand, glowing like it could taste the kill.

Now. This was her chance.

Haley leapt—blade raised, heart roaring.

The Athame struck deep behind its shoulders with a sickening *crunch*.

Still not the ear.

"Ray!" she gasped. "Tie its legs—now!"

Riya moved fast, vines snapping to life, wrapping the beast in a blur of green until it was pinned.

Haley lifted the Athame again, the blade shimmering with eerie intent— like it already knew where to strike.

She aimed behind its twisted ear—then froze.

Something shifted behind the Gloze's fixed stare—rising from deep within. It wasn't rage, or the malice the Rede had promised... but sorrow.

A shudder rippled through its chest, hard and glossy as a cockroach shell— and then it cried.

The sound was so small it broke Haley harder than any roar.

And in that moment, something inside her shifted—something that whispered she might be the only one left who could save it.

Then—

Riya screamed, "DO IT!"

But it was too late.

The vines snapped. The Gloze rose.

Round two had begun.

CHAPTER FORTY-TWO

HALLOWEEN

Haley bounced on the Gloze like it was a busted trampoline, slamming it into the jagged rocks.

Riya crouched behind a boulder, heart hammering. "Haley, kill it already!"

But Haley wasn't listening. She kept muscling the Gloze around, dodging beaks and fangs, but never going for the final blow.

Even with a perfect shot at its ear—the spot Inky swore would end it—Haley hesitated. Again.

"Haley!" Riya shrieked. "What are you doing?! STAB IT!"

"I know!" Haley shouted, dodging left as the Gloze swiped at her. "I'm just—processing!"

"WHAT?!"

Riya ducked behind a stalagmite, breath coming in hot gasps.

Haley clung to the beast's shoulders, muscles locked, like a cat mid-pounce, refusing to let go.

"Like—remember when we asked to see the truth?"

She drove her fist into the Gloze's head, then swung around its neck with the agility of a monkey. "I think I'm seeing things clearly for the first time. Or... maybe it's my powers?"

Riya clutched her curls like they were the only thing tethering her to reality.

"You're seriously having a feelings moment with a razor-handed death beast?!"

Haley backpedaled, knife still tight in her grip. "I'm serious! What if it's cursed? What if we're not supposed to kill it—what if we're supposed to save it?"

Riya gasped, like Haley had just grown a second head. "Save it?! Hales, it smells like roadkill microwaved in a haunted port-a-potty!"

The Gloze crouched low, trembling. Its ink-dark eyes shimmered—not with hunger, but with something worse. Something that looked a lot like grief.

Haley's eyes darted, frantic. "What if this is all a setup?! What if Inky's been feeding us Rede propaganda since day one?!"

"STOP MAKING UP CONSPIRACY THEORIES AND END THE MURDER-BIRD!"

The Gloze hissed and lunged again, and Haley barely dodged, hitting the ground in a roll.

Riya froze—her breath, her thoughts—just long enough to actually consider it.

Maybe Haley was right. The Athame was supposed to fly off and stab evil, right?

So why wasn't it doing anything now—when they needed it most?

The cave? Maybe.

Maybe their powers were glitching, or the rules had changed. But no.

Riya couldn't spiral. Not now. She had to hold it together—for both their sakes.

Haley needed to finish the mission. And Riya needed to get her out. Fast.

The cave was already working its twisted magic on Haley.

She circled the Gloze with a predatory sway, flinching and darting like a hungry lion toying with its kill—nothing like someone meant to end a demonic chicken.

"Listen," Riya said, her voice low and tight, like it was holding back a scream. "If we stay here any longer... you're going to turn into her."

Haley blinked. "Her who?"

"Her, her. Hexima."

A thin whistle slithered through the cave.

The shadows around them flickered. And then it started.

Haley's curls tightened into sharp ringlets. Her cheeks went gray-white. Her lips darkened to plum.

Riya stared. "Uh... Hales?"

"I'm fine," Haley muttered. "Just... watch."

She stepped forward, heart hammering, every instinct screaming to run. But she didn't.

Riya's breath caught—Haley was going to finish it, drive the Athame straight into the Gloze's ear.

The blade hummed, low and dangerous, its light pooling over the creature's jagged teeth.

Haley's arm drew back—and then, in a heartbeat that felt impossibly long, she twisted.

The Athame's glow flared as she drove it hard into the Gloze's chest. The creature let out a sound that wasn't a roar so much as a broken, shuddering cry—half fury, half pain.

Its body arched, spasmed. Black pus spilled from the wound, like ink reversing its fall, vanishing into the air before it touched the ground.

Riya's stomach lurched.

Haley stepped closer, the light gone from her eyes—murky now, like a pond left to rot.

She didn't just resemble Hexima. She was her.

That same wild, regal fury. That same quiet command, like a black hole swallowing light. A twin carved out of terror.

She held out the blood-slicked Athame.

"Use your Chemisource powers," she said. "Save it."

The knife dripped steadily, black pooling at her feet like a ticking clock.

Riya froze.

"Haley...?" Riya whispered.

But her cousin didn't blink—

"Save it," she whispered, the last light dying in her eyes. "Do it now. Or I end it. Both of you."

For a split second, Haley's eyes flashed violet.

Riya's chest tightened. This wasn't a joke. This wasn't a phase.

The Athame's point lifted, steady and deliberate, until Riya could see her own reflection warped in its black sheen.

Haley smiled.

But it wasn't her smile. It was too still. Too certain.

Riya knew, with a cold certainty, that she was no longer looking at her cousin.

But a more twisted version of Hexima.

CHAPTER FORTY-THREE

HALLOWEEN

Haley crawled toward Riya—slow, unblinking, all wrong.

Each movement jerked like a marionette yanked by invisible strings, as if something ancient had hijacked her skin and was fumbling through the memory of being human.

The Athame scraped beside her, its blade still slick, leaving a smear of black across the stone—thick, deliberate, glistening.

Riya's arms fell to her sides, powerless. She'd always followed the rules. Always played it safe.

But now? The rules had shifted—again.

The Gloze groaned, limbs twitching like a bug on its back. Its glassy eyes rolled, and in one last desperate lurch, it swatted Haley aside like she was nothing more than a discarded doll.

Then, dragging its withering body forward, the beast began to crawl—slow and relentless—right toward Riya.

Its chest gaped open, a mangled cavity of shadow and gore. And dangling from the wound like a charm on a chain—its heart.

Swinging. Beating. Still alive.

The Gloze crept closer and reached out—slow, uncertain—and rested a beak on Riya's shoulder. Gentle. Careful. Like a monster trying to ask for help.

Every cell in her body screamed to flinch, to run. But something deeper took over.

Her hands moved on their own, tracing symbols through the air in loops and arcs of light she didn't remember learning.

The glow from her palms spread through the Gloze's shadow-flesh, slick and uneasy—like oil skimming over water.

Then—blistering, blinding—heat.

It ripped through Riya's arms, through her ribs, through her soul. Her body pulsed—lit from within. The floor vanished. The cave screamed.

The Gloze arched back—

—then collapsed.

Still. Silent.

Its exposed heart slid back beneath the heavy armor of its chest—closing with the finality of a car door slamming in a storm.

Then—

A comet-green burst spiraled through the cave, wrapping the Gloze in living light.

Beaks softened into blunt fingers better made for hugs than harm, ridges melted to mossy blue skin that glowed faint as moonlight.

Its eyes, once feral, blinked slow and dazed—like waking from a nightmare.

And then its jaw unhinged... not to strike, but to smile. Crooked. Sloppy. Almost sweet.

Haley stirred, hair falling in soft, tight curls again, her cheeks blooming with a faint mauve flush. Lips warm. Natural. Alive.

Riya blinked, shaking off her powers like butterfly dust.

Haley was back—but the Gloze... was a whole new kind of terrifying.

It waddled toward them, tripping over a pebble. "Thanks, chu," it chirped in a squeaky megaphone voice. "My name's Rea. What's yours?"

Haley raised the Athame. "Stay back, Rea!"

The ogre lifted her oversized hands. "It's otay. I be nice. Take me to Zea? Pwease?"

She rocked from side to side like a cartoon hippopotamus.

Riya flinched.

"What now?" she hissed to Haley.

Before she could answer, lightning cracked above. Inky dropped from a tear in the ceiling and flipped to its final page.

Rea lurched forward.

"Oh, goodie! Me go now!" she clapped her gigantic hands.

"No, wait—" Riya dove for the book, but fog swallowed the cave before she could close it.

They blinked—and were back in Haley's bedroom.

So was Rea.

"...wee, wee, wee..." the ogre cooed, sitting cross-legged and tossing textbooks like paper airplanes.

The smell hit them—floral. And rotten.

Then—

Knock knock.

"Haley?" Raven called from the hallway. "Everything okay in there? Thought I heard... smelled... something."

Rea stood up and waddled toward the door.

Riya's eyes widened... They were so busted.

CHAPTER FORTY-FOUR

HALLOWEEN

Riya's heart plummeted right into her socks.

Footsteps. Just one. Slow. Deliberate. Each one landing like a countdown.

"NO!" she yelped, the word tearing out of her throat, panic shrieking through her like a fire alarm.

She vaulted across the room, snatching the comforter off the bed so fast it nearly took the pillows with it, and flung the blanket over Rea's enormous, egg-shaped head.

"Get in—get in—GET IN!" she hissed, her voice a frantic whisper that somehow felt louder than a scream.

Rea's eyes went wide and glassy.

The Gloze made a questioning grunt, but Riya was already shoving— her palms sinking into mossy skin, trying to wedge a creature the size of a refrigerator into a space meant for sweaters.

The closet groaned under the assault.

Rea's shoulder knocked down a hanger rod, a shoe skittered out and rolled across the floor, and her dopey arm flailed like she was waving for rescue.

"Almost—just—MOVE—" Riya gritted her teeth, giving one last desperate shove.

CLICK.

The latch caught.

"Hey, Mom!" Haley blurted, sudden and too bright, her voice the verbal equivalent of slamming on the brakes.

She planted her foot against the edge of the door, stopping it from swinging all the way open.

Riya's pulse thundered in her ears. From behind her, the comforter twitched.

Raven squinted into the room. "I thought I heard something. And it smells... weird. Like burnt garlic and... fur?"

"Pasta gas," Haley offered, clutching her stomach. "Or maybe internal combustion? We're still sick... kinda."

A muffled groan came from the closet.

Raven's brow arched. "What was that?"

"A-choo!" Haley fake-sneezed, voice crackly. "Still super contagious. CDC-level sick. Quarantine in progress. Please *and* thank you!"

Without waiting for a reply, Haley slammed the door shut.

She ripped the blanket away like it was an old bandage she couldn't stand to look at.

"Oh... lookie," Rea mumbled, blinking up from her cocoon, cheeks puffed like a sleepy toddler who'd just been told nap time was over. "Daytime again!" she chirped, her eyes glinting like two mismatched marbles.

"Ugh," Riya groaned, tossing the blanket aside. "This thing was supposed to be dead—now we're the ones about to be."

As if on cue, a faint rustle came from the corner. Socks shifted. A ripple of shadow darted out.

Inky slithered free, sleek and deliberate, snapping itself open mid-air before landing with a magical thud that rattled the floorboards.

Across its glitter-flecked pages, words erupted in furious bursts—spooling, spiraling, and looping as if it were screaming in cursive.

I AM FURIOUS WITH YOU TWO!

You ignored my instructions. You defied your destiny and the Fates. You risked everything!

And now, before I give you the worst news yet... Tell me: What. Exactly. Happened?!

Riya flinched. "There's worse news than this?" she muttered, pointing at the ogre drooling on Haley's carpet.

Haley cleared her throat, but her voice cracked anyway.

"Rea had a heart. Real tears. She wasn't evil—she was hurting."

She folded her arms, gaze hard.

"So yeah... you lied to us."

Inky flipped a page so fast it nearly tore, spattering ink into a miniature cyclone of sharp, slashing strokes.

212

Dearest Haley, you were fooled—not by me, but by your recklessness!
Queen Hexima's powers will peak tonight.
No one will join your fight. No army. No plan. NOTHING!
Except for a Shadow Gloze, which thinks pulling a blanket off its head means it's sunrise!
You did not weaken Queen Hexima... you freed her!
The Gloze is her Gatekeeper.
It guarded more than the threshold to the Veil—it bound Queen Hexima within.
Had you kept to the path—struck down the Gloze, taken the Light Oath, summoned the Light Veil—Queen Hexima's reign would have ended.
No war. No Shadow rising. No curse.
But now, the lock is broken. She walks free. Stronger than before.
And even now, she gathers her army.
Heed this—you cannot rewrite destiny by scrambling the order. I draw from both Veils. I see all paths.
You failed.

Haley stormed up to the book, fire blazing in her eyes.

"With my Zeno powers, I'll just undo this and redo it my way!"

A loud *snap* cracked through the room. Inky slammed shut, dust spiraling through the air like smoke from a gunshot.

Riya's voice came low and unsteady. "Hexima's probably halfway to our doorstep in a cloak made of our bad decisions."

Haley spun toward her—but Riya stood frozen, fists clenched, eyes burning with that dangerous flash.

"I can't keep doing this. With Inky. With you," she said, her voice cold enough to frost glass.

Haley blinked. "Wait... me? What did I do?"

"You made me believe we were in this together."

Her voice cracked, sharp and breaking all at once. "You went full villain in the cave—eyes glowing, knife raised like I was your enemy. You almost killed me, Hales. Me."

Her hands shook, fists half-formed. "You forced me to save that thing—whatever Rea even is now—and for what? To prove Inky wrong? To play hero?"

Riya's breath hitched. Her next words hit harder than a spell.

"I can't trust you anymore. You ruined everything."

Haley staggered like she'd been hit. "I'd never betray you! I just... I don't want to become *her*. So I tried to fix it my way."

213

Riya didn't blink.

Her eyes flicked to the photo on Haley's dresser—two muddy, grinning relics of who they'd been before cosmic doom and cursed responsibilities.

She looked away fast, jaw tight.

"There's no more *we*. I'm out."

Haley took a cautious step closer. "Please. We need each other. Rea might be able to help, too."

Riya flinched. "Seriously? Inky literally said not to do the steps out of order! And we don't even know if Rea's on our side!"

"Ray... I have a plan. A real one. No more winging it with magical heart surgery like what I just pulled off..."

A sheepish wince tugged at Haley's face. "Sorry for going rogue—and, uh... maybe a little evil."

"A plan? And a little evil?!" Riya barked, whipping toward her. "That wasn't tiny villain—it was full-mode scary! Do now, apologize later? What are you, five?"

"I'M SORRY!" Haley roared back, her voice cracking, the word ricocheting off the walls.

The fight drained from Riya's voice, replaced by something heavier—grief crashing in like a wave she couldn't outrun.

She sank onto the bed, pressing her fingers hard to her temples. Her skull throbbed. The room tilted, spinning in slow, nauseating circles.

And then—she froze.

Something was missing.

Something *big*.

CHAPTER FORTY-FIVE

HALLOWEEN

Raven's voice bounced upstairs as if it were on springs.

"Haley... Riya... get down here. Now!"

A pause. Then, louder—sharper:

"I THINK WE FOUND YOUR FRIEND!"

Riya's face contorted into a full-blown toad-like panic. "U-um, I don't think I can face our parents and ADMIT WE'VE BEEN LYING TO THEM THIS ENTIRE TIME!" she shrieked, panting like she'd just run a marathon made of guilt.

She spun in a frantic circle.

"The whole plan—thousands of years of secrets and ancient destinies— just *poof!* Gone. Vaporized. Up in mystical flames!"

Riya jabbed a finger toward Inky, who sat motionless on the floor like an innocent throw pillow.

"And *you!* You're just lounging there while reality melts faster than a popsicle in Dahmorte!"

Inky didn't so much as flutter a page.

"I'm serious!" she shouted. "We have a cursed ogre, a cosmic war on our doorstep, and my hair looks like it's been hexed by a tornado!"

She paced a tight loop, curls frizzing with every pass.

Haley lifted a hand, cautious. "So... we're just skipping the whole *forgiveness* part, then?"

"Seriously?" Riya snapped. "Jokes? That's your weapon of choice right now? We're about to be grounded into the next millennium—literally,

217

because, oh yeah, we're immortal—and there's a major magical disaster waiting downstairs!"

Haley's face collapsed into a half-moon frown.

No jokes this time. Just shame.

She'd failed—but not entirely. Saving the Gloze felt right. She still believed that…Mostly. She just needed time.

A *new* plan.

Anything other than standing around like a magical screw-up, dried blood under her fingernails, and no clue what came next. But time was a luxury she didn't have.

Downstairs, Raven's voice boomed again, slicing through the hallway like a thunderclap.

"GIRLS! NOW!"

Not the kind of tone that meant pancakes.

Haley swallowed hard. No more stalling.

She slipped the Athame into her sweatshirt pocket as Riya grabbed Inky, shoving it under her bulky clothes.

They turned the corner into the kitchen—and froze.

Rea sat at the dining table with her whole hand crammed into a cereal box far too small for her. She licked sugar-dusted fingers with fishy purple lips—slow, deliberate—like she was putting on glitter gloss for a funeral.

The cousins barely had time to exchange a look before they noticed their parents. Their eyes were bloodshot, faces drawn tight with exhaustion.

Raven's voice cut through the kitchen like the crack of a whip.

"Three. Days."

She took a slow step forward, toward the daughter who suddenly felt like a stranger. "You've been lying to us for three whole days."

The air suddenly felt too thin.

From the hallway, Xavier appeared, his frame filling the doorway. His expression was carved from stone, but his jaw worked like he was grinding his teeth to dust.

"Tell me your mother is exaggerating, Haley."

"She's… not," Haley admitted, lifting her chin as though bracing for impact.

Beside her, Riya shrank a little, arms wrapping around herself.

"Why?" Celeste's voice cracked—not with anger, but with fear. "Do you have any idea what we've been dealing with? You vanish without a word, leave traces of majick everywhere—" She stopped, pressing a hand to her temple like the words themselves hurt.

Riya flinched, her stomach knotting. "You think I wanted this?" The

218

words came out louder than she meant. "Every second, I've been trying to... I don't know... not die."

Celeste took a step forward, but Raven cut in first. "You're not the only ones who were *trying*," she said, her voice trembling now. "We've been holding the line for years—protecting you from dangers you can't even imagine."

Manchester's hands curled into fists. "And in three days, you've undone everything."

His gaze flicked between Riya and Haley, his deep voice trembling with restrained fury. "None of that matters now that you've brought a Gloze into Haley's house. What were you thinking?"

"I don't know," Riya blurted—too fast. "But I know what she means to Hexima and—"

"No, you don't," Raven snapped, stepping closer until she and Riya were almost nose-to-nose.

"That thing is Hexima's pet. The moment she realizes it's missing, she'll come for it—and for you."

For a moment, silence.

Just the hum of the fridge and Riya's uneven breathing.

Riya's head snapped up, tears bright in her eyes. "Then what are we supposed to do? Sit here and wait for Hexima to eat our heads off?!"

"You're supposed to trust us," Celeste shot back, her voice rising for the first time.

"I did! Until—oh, I don't know—three days ago, when we found out you've been lying to us our entire lives!" Riya snapped.

The air between them thrummed with tension, magic flickering faintly around the edges of the room.

Haley finally stepped in—far more confident than she should've been—sending alarm bells through her parents' bones.

"We can still fix this," she said firmly. "I can fix this."

Xavier barked out a humorless laugh. "Fix this? Do you have any idea what you've unleashed?"

Haley's voice sharpened. "I can use my Zeno powers—"

"This isn't a game!" Xavier roared, slamming his palm on the counter hard enough to rattle the mugs.

A faint shimmer of light cracked across the marble, magic sparking at the heat in his voice.

The overhead bulbs buzzed, shadows stretching along the walls like they were listening.

Then Raven's hand shot out, snatching the necklace from Haley's chest. "Where did you get this?!"

Haley flinched. "Queen Zion gave them to us."

Raven blinked, stumbling back into Xavier. "Queen Zion?" she whispered. "She—what? Without..." The last words faded, like a spell gone wrong.

Instant chaos.

Their parents erupted into curses and pacing, orbiting the kitchen island like angry moons.

Celeste paced harder than anyone, looping frantic circles like an ant that had lost the trail. "This is... this is not good," she chanted under her breath.

Her ivory fingers fidgeted in her pocket, brushing something that clinked faintly—like chainmail strung with pearls.

"That probably means you went to Aetherion Academy and—"

She stopped cold when both Riya and Haley nodded so hard their necks cracked.

"You're immortal now," she whispered, eyes shining with a strange mix of pride and heartbreak like a mom who'd missed her baby's first step... except this was their first cosmic rebirth.

Haley pulled the Athame from her sweatshirt like it was a graded test she expected praise for.

"Also, the Athame chose me," she said, voice tightening. "Me."

She reached for Riya, but Xavier stepped in front of her—hair shadowing his eyes, lips pressed tight, like he was swallowing a roar.

"No," he snapped, pointing a trembling finger. "That door's been sealed since before you were born. You took a weapon without permission!?"

"I didn't take it. Like I said—it chose me!" Haley shot back, heat rising in her voice.

Riya crossed her arms, chin lifting. "And I've got the Lumex now. So maybe rethink who's the 'weapon stealer.'"

Celeste looked like she might actually faint. "You're grounded—for eternity. Gloaming, remember? You can live forever—and we can ground you forever."

"We're calling Ama and Grandpa Henry," Raven added, already pulling out her phone like it was a wand of doom.

"Already texting," Celeste muttered, her thumbs flying with supernatural fury. "Group chat. Titled: *The Girls Blew Up the Universe.*"

Rea shifted, the floorboards creaking.

A low, confused grunt carried out of the kitchen.

"Can I pweze haz more crunchies?" Rea chirped. "Pwetty pweze?"

"NO!" everyone shouted at once.

Rea pouted, ears drooping, chin smushed against the table.

For a moment, no one spoke.

Then—faint but unmistakable—the sound of claws on wood.

It didn't belong in any room. Didn't belong in this world.

It came from outside the house.

The floorboards gave a low, shuddering groan, as if something vast had shifted in the morning dew.

A cold draft slid through the window seams, carrying the scent of wet earth and rust.

Low. Ancient. And very, very awake.

CHAPTER FORTY-SIX

HALLOWEEN

A bulging Shadow pressed against the window. For a moment—just the faint pop of splintering glass.

Then—CRASH.

The window exploded. Curtains thrashed, lights sputtered, chaos flooding the room.

The smell hit next—old wax, burnt wicks—before the dark poured in like spilled ink. In a blink, it rose, twisting into a hulking elephant of mist, eyes burning red through the haze.

"They're here," Manchester whispered, too late. "Elementals."

The Shadow thickened, sprouting claws that scraped the floorboards and three mouths gaping too wide to belong to any spirit. Cold bled from them, whispering promises of silence—of surrender.

Riya staggered back. Haley braced for a fight.

But before either could move, another voice thundered through the chaos—strong, commanding, impossible to ignore.

"Out."

Celeste stepped forward, palms outstretched, her hair snapping behind her in the unnatural wind. White fire burst from her hands, pure and searing, slicing through the Shadow's chest. Beside her, Raven was already chanting—low, guttural words.

The creature wailed, its scream like rusted hinges tearing apart. It tried to expand, to drown out the light, but their mothers only pressed harder.

"Leave this house. Now!" Celeste commanded.

The last of the darkness shrieked before it ripped free, sucked back through the shattered window like smoke into a storm.

And then—it was gone.

The air sagged heavy in the silence. Glass glittered across the floor.

Celeste turned, her face pale but fierce. "This is only the beginning. She'll keep sending them until the curse is broken."

Raven's voice dropped to a whisper. "And next time, she won't settle for shadows."

Then—Manchester spoke. His voice was low, reluctant, cracking at the edges.

"*The Book of Fates* warned us long ago... if the steps weren't completed in the right order—and before this birthday—"

He paused, fingers twisting his lucky blue tie. Riya's stomach dropped—he only touched it when things were truly bad.

"Then Hexima could take your onus—your souls—forever."

Tears stung Riya's eyes.

The thought of losing their souls—of battling more nightmares—punched the breath from her chest. She shrank inward, small as a mouse.

"How did we not know about this part, Dad?" she snapped. "That feels like a pretty important detail to skip."

Manchester let out a long, exhausted sigh. "It wasn't a secret. You had everything in front of you—The book, the weapons, the potions. But you didn't ask. You didn't want to know."

Celeste stepped in, her voice gentler. "Remember those mini chocolate muffins I used to make when you were sad? They're majickal. *Screaming-nettle cakes*. I made them with the screeching toads in the attic."

Riya recoiled. "Ew. Like... with body parts? Mom?!"

"No, sweetie," Celeste said calmly. "I'd bake the muffins first—then squeeze the toad over them while it screamed. The sound sealed the spell. Whoever ate it got twenty-four hours of protection... and happiness."

Riya gawked. "So we're basically doomed because we didn't ask the right questions, and we like dessert?! Are you hearing how insane this sounds?!"

She threw up her hands. "Unreal."

Riya stepped beside Haley in the kitchen, away from the others, shoulders squared with something sharper than anger—clarity.

Haley had told the truth. Their family hadn't. The real enemy was everyone else.

When Riya spoke, her voice was low and rough, like rocks sliding over steel.

"Lying to us is way worse than anything Haley's pulled. Even going all evil

224

in a cave—or, you know, lying for a few days." She shot Raven a sharp side-eye.

Haley blinked, surprised, then reached for Riya's hand. "Thanks."

"Don't mention it," Riya muttered. But her grip didn't loosen.

Raven swooped around the chair like an eagle spotting a mouse.

"Enough!" she roared. "Your onus are in great danger, and that Gloze will betray you. Get rid of her and take the oath. Now."

Rea growled low, the sound rumbling through the floor. "Me a Lightwice now! ME STAY!"

"Leave, ogre," Raven barked.

"NO!"

Rea hurled the kitchen table like a Frisbee. It crashed against the wall, missing the coffee machine by inches, which Raven silently thanked the stars for.

Then Rea balanced two stools on her shoulders and vaulted upward, spearing them into the ceiling like she was installing a chandelier—decorating with pure chaos.

Raven shrieked, "You can't destroy our kitchen just because you got your feelings hurt!"

Rea growled, one foot planted in a crater of linoleum.

"That's ENOUGH, beast!" Raven snapped, her voice shaking with fury. "I hope you explode—because you're still EVIL, no matter how many group hugs you've had!"

Rea stormed in front of the cousins like a blue, puddy shield.

"These are me friends... go away," she said, her voice crackling like a busted speaker trying to sound polite.

To Riya, Rea was still a walking red flag. But Haley saw something else—possibility. That even something molded from Shadow could change.

If Rea could be remade, then maybe she could, too.

Shadow didn't have to mean doom.

For a heartbeat, Rea wasn't a monster—she was the big sister they hadn't known they needed.

But to the cousins' parents, she was terror given shape—horror molded in a ton of blue clay.

"Honey," Raven whispered, her voice cracking. "Please. Make the Gloze leave. For all our sakes."

Haley's throat tightened. She looked at Rea—hulking, confused, almost endearing—and then back at her mom.

"I'm sorry," she said, voice trembling but firm. "She stays. And... I think I have a *new* plan."

Defiance steadied her. She took Rea's hand—slow, deliberate.

"She stays," she said, low and unshakable.

Silence cracked for half a second.

Riya felt it—the shift. Fearlessness rolling off Haley, sparking that same surge of courage in her.

Her voice came out fire-wrapped velvet—steady, burning.

"Haley's right. Rea stays."

Gasps cracked the air, but Riya didn't flinch.

"I healed her. With my power. And unless the universe is suddenly in the business of blessing evil, soul-sucking monsters..." Her gaze swept the room like a blade. "She's not one."

Her gaze swept the room, eyebrows raised. "Or should I ignore the magical miracle because it's inconvenient to everyone's opinion?"

Manchester's face twisted in disbelief, fury barely contained. "This has gone too far. You're still just kids!"

"Too far for what?" Haley snapped, her voice ice-cold and rising like a storm swell. "For saving something you call a monster, but was just hurting? For not blindly following the rules you never even explained?"

Xavier stepped forward, jaw locked. "That's it. We're calling the Rede."

Haley didn't flinch. "Go ahead. Do it. While you're at it, tell them we've got Rea now. And we're just getting started. We'll find the others—everyone they left behind."

That stopped him cold.

"The others?" he repeated, voice low and curling like dry ice vapor. "Who exactly are you talking about?"

The room held its breath.

Spells paused mid-flight, glowing like suspended lightning. A ward circle on the floor fizzled, unfinished.

Even Ama stopped chanting—her lips parted, her palms hovering above a bowl of moon salt.

Riya and Haley shared a glance—equal parts dread and defiance.

Then Haley stepped forward.

The flicker of doubt in her eyes burned off like the morning fog.

"The ones like us," she said softly. "The ones your Rede left behind. The ones who survived anyway."

A pulse of something ancient stirred under her skin. Her hands curled into fists at her sides.

"The ones who remember what was taken. Who knows what's coming."

She smiled then—fierce, reckless, unstoppable.

"The ones who are ready to watch Hexima burn."

CHAPTER FORTY-SEVEN

HALLOWEEN

Riya ducked as a cursed candlestick spun past her ear, shrieking like a tiny banshee. She swatted it away with a dishcloth and spun toward Haley.

This wasn't just chaos. It was war prep disguised as a family meltdown.

"Do we have a plan for when the adults actually combust? Like—physically catch fire?"

"No... but," Haley shouted back, "I'm working on it!"

"Work faster!" Riya snapped, her curls sparking with static.

Ama was warding the windows with sigils made of salt and ash.

Henry was shouting into an orb that refused to connect.

Riya and Haley slipped into the corner of the kitchen as Rea lumbered after them, swatting at the flickering light still swinging from where she'd knocked it loose with the overturned stools, muttering like it was hexed.

Riya caught her thick hand and tugged it down. "It's a bulb, not a demon."

Then, lowering her voice, eyes flicking to Haley.

"I think we can still do the steps... just not their way. Ours," Riya said.

"YES!" Haley grinned.

"No screw-ups this time," Riya warned.

"Deal."

Haley laid out the new plan: Light Oath, Dahmorte, Everbind... army.

Their parents were still arguing, but there was no time to listen.

Haley pulled out the Athame.

Riya gagged. "Do we seriously have to slice our actual palms? Like, with

229

blood?"

Haley didn't answer. She just dragged Rea closer, her jaw set like concrete.

The Athame gleamed in her grip.

Rea frowned. "Rea, no like paper cuts..."

Riya winced, eyeing the knife. "This is more like a 'congrats, you're in a blood cult' kind of cut, sweetie."

But Haley's grip didn't waver. "No backing out now."

She raised the blade. Riya and Rea held their breath.

Behind them, their family kept hurling spells like toddlers in a food fight—messy, loud, and wildly off-target.

The kitchen air curdled, magic turning sour like spoiled cream. An omen was forming—demonic, wrong in every way.

And with no adult supervision in sight, the tension dripped like frosting sliding off a cursed cake.

Haley raised the blade like every reckless witch in a bad horror movie—too slow, too dramatic, and definitely not parent-approved.

Riya muttered, "Great. Nothing says family bonding like voluntary blood loss."

Steel touched skin with a cold hiss, patient and hungry, as if it had been waiting centuries for a choice like this.

CHAPTER FORTY-EIGHT

HALLOWEEN

Haley went first—*shhk.*

The blade slid. The cut was real. And so was the ancient magic crawling up her arms—prickling, relentless, like ants on espresso.

Riya hissed as Haley followed up with hers, jaw locked, the sting flashing hot.

"Ow," she groaned.

The blade practically purred in Haley's hands, smug and satisfied, like a cat after cream.

Next was Rea. She whimpered like a small dog but didn't flinch, holding out her trembling hand as the blade split her thick skin.

The air filled with the metallic tang of blood—laced with something faintly, disturbingly sweet.

Three cuts. Three heartbeats.

Blood pooled together—Riya's and Haley's a deep, human red, while Rea's shimmered blue, swirling as if it had a pulse of its own.

Haley blinked. "Um... isn't it supposed to be, like, black slime?"

Riya stayed silent, her face drained of color, eyes locked on Rea's blood. It was beautiful—like a tiny tropical ocean blooming in their kitchen—but wrong.

Her throat bobbed; she looked like she might puke.

Haley side-eyed Riya.

"Do you need some apple juice?" she asked.

Riya blinked. "I'm literally leaking blood."

"Low blood sugar?"

"It's a wound, Hales—not a snack break."

"Okay," Haley hissed back. "Then let's get a move on with the next step—"

"I know, the Light Oath," Riya muttered, still reeling from the knife's slice.

They pressed their palms together.

Riya and Haley spoke in unison, their voices low and steady.

> *By blood we bind,*
> *With Light we shine,*
> *Our Fates forever intertwined*

The room pulsed.

Haley felt the shift—something pulling from Shadow into Light—but she didn't dare lose momentum. Still, the words stalled on her tongue.

She blinked. "Okay... I totally blanked on the next part. You and your freaky memory got it covered, or...?"

"I got it," Riya said, steady now, though her hand still trembled in Haley's.

> *By blood and bond, by pain and power,*
> *We vow beneath this sacred hour—*
> *To guard the Light, to fight the dark,*
> *To leave no soul without a spark.*
> *Let Shadow know our names with fear,*
> *Let majick mark us ever near.*

Then... nothing.

"I said it right!" she insisted.

Suddenly—*pop.*

The air crackled. Every light bulb in the house flickered, dimmed, then buzzed back to life with a twitchy hum.

Riya and Haley froze, expecting that by now their family would be on full magical-guardian duty—complete with shouting, ward-raising, and the usual meltdown over their teenage rebellion.

But no.

The adults kept slinging spells like lassos and yelling at each other, so wrapped up in their own chaos that the kitchen—and the blood on the floor—went completely unnoticed.

It struck Riya as... odd.

"This is either the best diversion we've ever pulled off," she said flatly, "or the end of everything."

"I don't know why it didn't work, though," Haley said. "I know you did it right and—"

Ding.

Riya jumped. "What was that?!"

Another low *thunk* echoed from the corner of the kitchen.

They turned in unison.

Finally, Riya set Inky on the counter and walked toward the ajar pantry door.

A faint, eerie glow seeped through the cracks like moonlight leaking from another dimension.

Haley crept forward, the Athame still in hand. "Please don't be a poltergeist. Please don't be a poltergeist."

There, crammed between a box of stale cereal and a sack of potatoes—stood Rea—radiating light like a humanoid flashlight on full beam. Her eyes glowed white-hot, pupils vanished entirely.

"Oh my stars," Riya whispered. "She's gone full glow worm."

Rea blinked slowly. "Rea... feel funny."

"You're in the pantry," Haley said, baffled.

"Rea got hungry," she admitted, shrugging as her glowing arm reached toward a bag of marshmallows.

The marshmallow bag combusted with a soft *puff* of smoke and smelled like a smore gone evil.

Haley dropped her head into her hands. "Okay, so maybe the Light Oath did something. Like... supercharged her."

"Or turned her into a radioactive fridge ghost," Riya muttered.

Riya waved a hand in front of Rea's face.

Nothing.

The ogre was locked in a wide-eyed, glowing-eyed daze.

"Strange," Riya muttered. "She was all there like five seconds ago."

Haley tilted her head. "Should we... use her as a flashlight or something?"

Riya shot Haley a look that screamed, *No—for all we know, she could still combust.*

But Rea was already moving. Stiff. Trance-like. Straight to Inky.

Without hesitation, she lifted the book high above her head, holding it like a crown meant for a queen.

CRACK.

The cover split down the spine. Pages fluttered like dying wings.

Riya gasped. "She actually killed Inky. Like, for real!"

235

Haley's heart slammed against her ribs. "What!?" She bolted toward the glowing beast. "Put that down!"

Then—without warning—Rea lunged forward and scooped them up like lunchboxes, one cousin dangling under each arm.

They jolted in her grip, the scent of moss and woodsmoke clinging to her skin.

"No—wait—" Riya shrieked.

But it was too late.

Rea hurled Inky to the floor. It hit with a sickening *thwack*, flailing like a dying bird—pages twitching, trying to stitch itself back together.

Riya gasped. It felt like a gut punch.

But Inky wasn't done yet.

With a final shiver, it flung itself to a single, glowing page.

"Wait—" Riya choked, reaching out.

Poof.

A flash of white-hot light spread through the room like honey.

And just like that—Rea. Riya. Haley. Gone.

Sucked into the book like water down a drain.

Inky snapped shut with a final, echoing *click*.

Silence fell.

The book curled inward and burned at the edges before extinguishing itself in a puff of smoke and laughter.

CHAPTER FORTY-NINE

HALLOWEEN

The cousins hit with a wet *splat*, sinking into black sludge—thick and sucking, like rotten eggs left in a sauna or something long dead that had forgotten its own name.

It was a place *where death went to die.*

"Ugh! EW! GROSS!" Riya shrieked, flailing toward the nearest rock-like shape—only to realize it moaned and slithered away.

She froze. "I have goo in my socks. It's warm. Why is it warm?!"

Haley emerged next, covered head to toe in gunk, blinking slowly like a dazed cryptid. "Is this... Dahmorte?" she croaked.

Riya clutched her sludge-soaked hoodie like it was the last scrap of her dignity.

"Yep. Pretty sure it's exactly what you asked for," she deadpanned.

Then something howled in the distance—low, dissonant, like a wolf gargling gravel.

Haley stiffened. "Y'know, for a death realm, this place is kinda... extra."

"You mean besides the goo-pit entrance, and the haunted wind?"

Haley pointed behind. "And that."

Dozens of glowing red eyes blinked open in the darkness—watching.

The cousins froze. Something shifted beyond the fog. Not a flicker. Not a shadow. Something massive.

Out of the haze, Rea emerged—looking far too pleased with herself. Steam curled from her glowing skin. Her eyes pulsed silver, and her grin—wide as a conch shell—made her round cheeks gleam like twin moons.

239

"So…" Haley coughed, still spitting muck, "Rea might be evil after all?"

Riya scraped ooze off her face, only to smear it deeper into her already funeral-worthy frown lines.

"Oh, you mean our ogre pal who just used a half-possessed murder journal as a ride to… you know… here? Yeah, super subtle. Almost as sneaky as a marching band at a funeral."

With a loud *snap*, Rea lunged toward the twisted trees, and the cousins stumbled after her, jittery and dazed, struggling to match her massive stride.

Shadows clung like cobwebs, snagging their hair and clothes as Haley tightened her grip on the Athame—her palm still burning from the oath-cut, a deeper ache twisting in her gut, as if this place already knew her name.

Riya shot her a wary glance. "You okay? You've got that 'Haley's-about-to-go-full-villain' face again."

"I'm fine," Haley snapped—too quickly.

The ground shuddered beneath them.

Dahmorte had felt their arrival.

Claws scraped stone in the dark, and from the fog ahead—something growled back.

CHAPTER FIFTY

HALLOWEEN

Back in the kitchen—somewhere between wrangling Inky over a bubbling death soup and the Lightwice family officially losing their grip on witch reality—a soul-rattling wail erupted from the book, shaking the windows in their frames.

It had never sounded like that before—part squeaky dog toy, part stadium speaker being tortured in slow motion.

The Lightwices froze.

For a breath, they weren't protectors—they were bullies, turning on an unarmed, if maddeningly uncooperative, book.

But with doom pressing closer by the second, the adults were ready to strike at anything that stood between them and their girls.

Even Inky.

"This isn't working!" Celeste snapped, breath ragged. "We need another way to reach the girls—the book's silent, and we're out of time for it to start talking."

She froze mid-breath, eyes widening. "Oh, my stars... wait."

She pulled a pink rose quartz crystal from her pocket, the kind used to unlock secret spells. "What about Unlock-with-a-Knock? It worked on candy shop doors when we were kids—might work on the book without damaging it." She frowned. "But I'll need an amethyst instead."

Good thing Raven kept her crystals charging in the spice cabinet.

Celeste reached in, fingers closing around the purple stone—when her foot slid on something slick. Her leg shot out like a cheerleader mid-kick, arms

243

flailing until she flushed red and hissed, *"Go up and stay up!"*

"Uh... guys?" she croaked. "You're gonna want to see this."

Still hovering inches off the floor, she pointed down. "That's Hive's blood..." Her voice thinned to a whisper.

Beneath her, a shimmering pool glowed aqua-bright in the kitchen light.

Ama crouched, dabbing the liquid with a napkin. She flicked her wrist. "Whose blood is this?"

From the folded napkin, a tiny, orange-winged fairy no bigger than a dragonfly wriggled free. Its face—creased like the bark of an ancient tree—knotted deeper as it sniffed the blood.

"The Gloze's," it whispered.

Ama's eyes narrowed. "Try again."

The fairy dipped one toe into the pool. Blue light flared—searing, blinding—and swallowed it whole. When it dimmed, a radiant young man stood in its place, skin aglow, hair streaked with starlight.

He turned, eyes blazing like twin comets, and sang in a voice that rang like a church bell, "The Gloze—it's saved!"

Then it fluttered out the window in a puff of glitter.

Ama handed the napkin to Xavier. "The girls were right," she whispered. "Riya saved Rea. That blood—it confirms everything."

Xavier held the cloth up to the light.

The shimmer wasn't natural—blue like crushed sapphires, pulsing faintly in the kitchen's dim glow.

But his eyes darkened.

"Even if they saved that beast," he muttered, "they're not safe. Not yet."

Without flinching, Xavier leaned in and snarled at the napkin—feral, protective, like an animal guarding its young.

Raven arched a brow, startled but sly. "Wow," she purred, batting batting a trained eyelash. "Haven't heard you roar in ages."

He shot her a look that was half love, half jagged guilt—the kind born of failing to protect the one thing they both loved most: Haley.

Steam curled from the cauldron of Devil's Goo, brewed from hunks of devil's claw—roots like shriveled baby monkeys clutching cactus spines, ghost fingers beckoning him closer.

"They said they were going to find 'the others,'" he muttered, jaw tight. "Hexima's castoffs. Whatever rejects are still rotting in Everbind."

A beat of silence. The air thickened.

His voice dropped, low and certain. "The Limbo Veil. Harshmoon's domain. The only way in... is through Dahmorte."

Manchester stepped forward—calmer than Xavier, but no less dangerous.

He fixed the book with a hard stare. "Then we get them back," he said. "Before it's too late."

Because far from the kitchen—far from safety—Riya and Haley were already too deep to crawl out.

And something was waiting at the bottom.

CHAPTER FIFTY-ONE

HALLOWEEN

Down in Dahmorte's twisted swamp, figures emerged—twitchy, distorted things with skin like melting wax and eyes that blinked sideways.

One dragged a leg like a broken puppet. Another had no mouth at all.

"Hales," Riya whispered, backing into Rea, "are these friends of yours?"

"I think... I think they're Hexima's rejects," Haley murmured.

"You mean like her evil exes?"

"No. Like failed creations. Broken Maldrops."

Riya winced as one squelched closer. "Yeah, that's not better."

The tallest creature let out a rattling hiss—then sank to one knee before Haley, head bowed in eerie reverence.

One of the beasts coiled around her feet, purring low like a mutton cat—a sound that landed somewhere between a kitten's hum and the growl of something that had eaten a kitten.

Rea stepped forward. "They see new queen."

She pointed at Haley—slow, deliberate—like spotting a spider crawling across the ceiling.

"They think I'm... her," Haley whispered.

"WHAT?!" Riya shrieked.

She took a gigantic step back. "Okay, not gonna lie. You're giving serious dark empress vibes right now... and not the fun kind."

Behind them, something *snapped*.

Haley froze.

Half-buried in the muck, a black stone throbbed like a living heart. Its glow matched her amulet and the Athame—only colder. Hungrier.

She pointed. "Rea. What is that?"

Rea's eyes widened. For the first time, she looked reverent—afraid, even—like life had flickered back into her.

"That's *Moonglade Stone*," Rea whispered, her voice heavy as a dropped anchor. "Trap stone. Keeps Maldrop in. Very old. Very cursed. Only for high darklings."

High darklings?

Riya gulped. "Wow. Sounds super charming."

Rea tilted her head. "Harshmoon leads. But must accept."

Riya shoved Haley with her elbow. "Accept what—like a monster internship?"

Haley's gaze hardened. "We need help, Riya. If the Light realm won't back us... we build our own. These creatures could be it."

Riya threw up her hands. "Okay, building a Maldrop army is one thing—but joining them? That's a whole new brand of crazy!"

And then, without a word, Haley dropped to her knees.

Riya flailed. "Dude! Don't touch it! That thing's screaming bad idea in, like, twelve languages!"

"I have to know," Haley whispered.

Her fingers brushed the surface. Power exploded through her like a thunderclap. The creatures shrieked in unison.

Riya yanked her back. "Nope! Nope-nope-nope. This is literally how villains get born. We are unplugging your spooky rock phase."

A sudden *thawp* split the air, sharp enough to cut through their pounding hearts.

They spun—ready for teeth or claws—only to freeze at the sight of something far worse.

High on a jagged ridge, a black castle loomed—its thorn-tangled turrets clawing at a bruised sky.

Riya's breath faltered. "Tell me that's not Hexima's place."

"Yup," Haley said, eyes locked on the spires. "Evil Barbie Dreamhouse."

The twisted trees vomited hundreds of potbellied, shrieking birds into the night sky. They swarmed like hissing bats, blotting out the lavender moon in a frenzy of wings.

Riya clambered onto Rea's thigh—massive and warm, like a boulder wrapped in shag carpet—just in time to dodge a demon clawing out of a shallow grave.

She screamed, "One of them just breathed on me! It smells like haunted hot dogs!"

248

"Haley!" she hissed. "We need a new plan. Fast!"

"Yeah," Haley muttered. "Let's go before this turns into the next big hit— *The Hexima Saga*."

Together, the cousins and Rea stepped forward.

Toward the portal.

Toward Everbind.

But just before crossing, Haley glanced back. The Moonglade Stone still pulsed.

Without a word, she slipped it beneath her sweatshirt.

The burn started soft, then burrowed deeper—pressing against her stomach like a second heartbeat.

No turning back. The Light no longer held the only claim to her. And the Shadow... was starting to feel like home.

They stepped through—swallowed by a curtain of Shadow. Thick. Cold. Hungry.

Then—like venom through a vein—a voice slithered up behind them.

"Welcome," it purred. "To my kingdom."

CHAPTER FIFTY-TWO

HALLOWEEN

A giant figure stepped from the shadows—winged, scaled, unnaturally perfect.

Lion thighs. Snake torso. Ridiculous abs.

Riya gawked. Haley froze.

"Long before your first breath," the creature purred, "I knew your mothers. They dared steal what was mine."

It slithered closer, gliding across the ground like mercury on a glass surface.

"I am Harshmoon," he intoned, staff gleaming with coiled serpents. "Kneel before me."

Harshmoon wasn't just dangerous; he was madness caged in flesh, waiting to spring like a starving tiger.

One moment his eyes were storm-cloud black, bottomless and deadly; the next, they burned with a flame so hypnotic it promised beauty and ruin in the same breath.

Riya squinted. Her heart was hammering, but her mouth ran anyway.

"Yeah, no. Fun fact—we don't do bowing," she stammered.

Silence snapped into a command: "KNEEL — or I will rip your onus out through your nose!" Harshmoon thundered.

Haley slid forward like a shadow, voice flat and sure. "So—where do we find the rest of your undead?"

Harshmoon's eyes snagged on her hand.

"The Athame?" His voice scraped like steel on bone. "Stolen by your mothers, remembered by the Fates. And now a child dares to wave it? History does not favor children. It devours them."

A twitch broke his mask.

"I should tear your sight from your sockets," he intoned, "and give it to my beasts—let them dine on your last vision."

Behind him, two monstrous wolverines lowered their heads, fangs flashing—ears perking as if someone had just said the word *snack*.

Riya recoiled. Haley... did not.

She met his storm-swept gaze without flinching. The Athame had chosen her—Fate-bound steel doesn't betray its keeper.

With a confidence she had no right to own, Haley drifted closer, like the space itself belonged to her.

"Haley, no!" Riya barked. "Step away from the criminally hot, evil man!"

Haley turned, and the look she gave wasn't rebellion. Wasn't defiance. It was peace—like she'd just found a lost childhood teddy bear reborn as a gorgeous beast, swinging a lamppost-sized scepter like it was weightless.

Even Riya felt the pull—but she clamped onto Haley's arm, hard.

"We stick to the plan," she hissed. "Remember?"

Haley slipped free, gliding toward Harshmoon, who reached out as if greeting a daughter.

Then—CRACK. His serpent staff slammed down, the sound rattling bone. Shadows split, and the monsters slithered forward—hungry, twitching.

Haley just batted her lashes.

"Holy H," Riya muttered.

This was bad. *Really bad.*

CHAPTER FIFTY-THREE

Halloween

In the folds of Everbind's rot-thick fog, the wind whispered wagers—Haley's ruin already the favored bet.

Inky had warned her: too much Shadow, and she wouldn't just flirt with danger—she'd belong to it.

Now, with every step she took toward Harshmoon, that warning no longer felt like prophecy. It was becoming fact.

Riya saw it too, but she had no time to dwell on Haley's unraveling—Haley was about to do something wildly dangerous, verging on deranged.

Haley didn't think. She moved.

Thud.

The Moonglade Stone struck the ground with finality—like a coffin slamming shut on destiny.

For a heartbeat, silence reigned. Then she twirled the Athame between her fingers, a small, cracked grin spreading—something fit for a clown who'd lived too long under a bridge.

And before anyone could stop her, she drove the Athame into the stone.

The High Darkling had arrived—and she let the black slime hiss up the blade, wet and serpentine, coiling around her hand.

The beasts shrieked. Harshmoon buckled.

"P-please," Harshmoon gasped.

He writhed like a dying fish, words spilling in ragged surrender. "We will stand beside you... only grant us mercy... as you will it."

Behind her, Riya shouted.

"Haley, STOP!" Riya shouted, panic spiking hard enough to sting her throat. "They said they're on our side!"

She lunged for her cousin, but Haley caught her mid-stride, pinning her with effortless, almost inhuman strength.

One more flick—just one—and she could end them all. Annihilation balanced on her fingertips.

Haley's grip was ice and iron, her expression locked in something halfway between a snarl and a smile.

Her lips barely moved.

"Riya... help me."

And then the light was gone again, swallowed by the shadow boiling off her skin.

Riya's heart slammed against her ribs.

She didn't know who to save first—Haley or Harshmoon—until the sight in front of her yanked every hair on her arms straight up.

Haley's eyes burned violet, pupils fractured into shards of Shadow.

"Haley..." Her voice cracked, thin and frayed. "You have to stop. Don't do—"

The rest died on her tongue.

Because the thing wearing Haley's face tilted its head, the Athame pulsing in her grip like a pet.

The Maldrops whimpered, clutching one another, their small bodies smeared with dark blood and grime. They weren't warriors, weren't enemies— just victims caught in the fracture of Haley's insatiable thirst for Shadow power.

Riya's chest seized.

Decide now.

She slammed her palm to the ground, Chemisource Light flaring through her like wildfire.

She chanted the Light Oath, loud.

> *By blood we bind*
> *With Light we shine*
> *Our Fates forever intertwined*

A spark flared from the scar on Riya's neck—sharp, electric—and she lit up like a torch against the violet sky.

She didn't understand what was happening—until Haley snapped upright as if yanked from tar. Then she grinned—warm cinnamon lips, mischief blazing.

256

Back, like nothing had happened.

The Maldrops froze mid-lunge. Their snarls faltered. Pupils blew wide, like they were seeing for the first time.

Claws uncurled into rough, human hands. Fangs slipped back. Slime hissed off their skin.

One blinked, eyes big and wet as a puppy's. Another cracked a slow, crooked grin—like a turtle waking from a nap.

They didn't disappear. They changed.

Harshmoon shed his scales in slow, deliberate layers. When he rose, he stood tall—regal, otherworldly.

He dropped to one knee, lowering his serpent staff with devotion. His voice was clear and specific.

"We kneel in oath... to Queen Haley, Sovereign of Shadow, and Princess Riya, Keeper of The Light."

In that breath, the war's current course changed.

The cousins, Rea, and their unlikely army marched toward the cave, vines sparkling and silver mist curling around them.

Behind them, the Maldrops joked:

"When I find Hexima, I'm squeezing her like a tube of toothpaste!"

"—and swinging her by her spongy hair into the void."

Laughter echoed.

The cousins couldn't help but smile—until they stepped through the portal...

...and landed hard—a football field away from where the Charmwic Ball should've been.

Riya blinked, then turned to Haley.

"Um... Hales," she whispered. "This can't be good."

CHAPTER FIFTY-FIVE

HALLOWEEN

The sun sagged low in a strawberry-stained sky, teetering on the edge of the old church steeple like it was about to take its final bow.

Dusk bled in fast—too fast—spilling across the field like black ink flooding a page.

A thin laugh slipped out of Riya's cracked lips, but it died quickly—cut off by the tremor in her hands. She jabbed a finger toward the ridge, shaking.

"Okay, but seriously—look." Her voice wavered, cracking under its own weight. "We saved the Maldrops, but..."

She didn't finish. She didn't have to.

Over the hill, stretching farther than the eye could see, rows of crystal-like figures blazed in formation.

Riya's mouth dropped. "Uh... yeah. So, remember when I guessed no one would come?"

She jabbed a finger toward the horizon as it split open—a tide of halos, wings, and burning eyes. The ground quaked beneath their march, dust curling upward like fresh storm clouds.

"Yeah, try *all* of them." Her voice cracked, half-laugh, half-sob. "We are so far over our little witch heads right now."

Then it came. Footsteps.

Faint at first, then growing.

Not rushed.

Not panicked.

Deliberate.

Closing in.

Riya and Haley groaned in unison.

"Please," Riya muttered, "no more surprises."

Too bad. This one was unavoidable.

She turned—and froze. Their parents were there, silent and sudden, like the Shadows had smuggled them in.

"Mom?" Riya squinted. "What... are you wearing?"

At first glance, it looked like Halloween costumes—until the dying light caught the edges, making the leather gleam and the metal studs pulse faintly, like they were breathing.

"The Fates' armor," Celeste declared, fastening the buckles of her knife belt with the precision of someone who had done it a thousand times before. Her dark brown eyes burned—not soft, not motherly, but sharp as forged steel.

She unsheathed a blade, its edge singing in the dying light.

"We fight for the Light!"

Then—Manchester's battle cry ripped through the air, so deep it seemed to rattle the dirt beneath their feet.

"Dad?" Riya's laugh came out thin, a brittle thing dressed as humor. "I swear I just died of secondhand embarrassment."

Celeste stepped forward, arms stacked with neatly folded leather and gear.

"Oh wow," Riya said, faking cheer. "Matching outfits. Just what every daughter dreams of before battle."

That's when the sound came—low and unnatural.

A whistle, but wrong.

"Riya," Celeste barked, her eyes burning with the fire of a general long buried but never broken. "The Lumex is yours. Wield it as if the world depends on it—because it does."

Raven and Xavier weren't far behind—strapping layer after layer of the same war-gear onto Haley until she staggered beneath its weight.

Riya hesitated, voice small against the clash of buckles and steel. "What about Inky?"

Celeste's head snapped toward her, eyes blazing.

"Here," she said, forcing the book into Riya's arms. "Guard it—please. Promise me you'll stay safe." Her voice broke. "We can't go any further... this is your fight now."

Riya's throat tightened, but she nodded once—no words, no hesitation.

She tucked Inky under one arm, as if it had always belonged there.

Ama and Henry rounded the corner, both riding matching white unicorns.

Riya's eyes widened. "Wait... nobody said anything about unicorns."

She beamed. "Okay, I might be interested in this fight now."

But Ama—calm and unshakable in a brown leather catsuit—shook her head.

"No, sweetie. These are for us. You'll stay grounded and protect the book like your life depends on it. Scratch that—the universe depends on it."

The words landed heavy, too heavy, settling in Riya's chest like stones.

Haley let out a scoff that sounded sharper than it should've. "No pressure, right, Ray?"

As quickly as their family had arrived, they vanished—no hugs, no goodbyes, just war in their wake.

Wartime was here.

CHAPTER FIFTY-SIX

HALLOWEEN

Riya's stomach flipped so many times she lost count.

The quiet left in the wake of their family riding off into the sunset—on *literal unicorns*—wasn't comforting. It pressed in heavily, buzzing with everything unsaid, loud in all the wrong ways.

Her thoughts scattered wild, vicious, tearing into each other like feral cats clawing for the same exit. No order. No focus. Just panic with teeth.

Haley caught it, like scent on the wind.

"You okay?"

"No," Riya muttered. "I look like a wannabe gladiator stuffed in a sausage casing. Exactly the vibe I was going for before battle."

"This is not gonna be easy," Haley said, voice bitter.

"What won't?" Riya asked, bracing for the doom prediction.

"Getting everyone on our side," Haley answered, jaw tight. "If we don't, we're done."

"Okay—but how?" Riya bit her chapped lip.

Haley opened her mouth... then shut it again, like two frozen fish sticks refusing to part.

Riya raised a brow. "Did your brain just freeze?"

Classic Haley—more instinct than plan.

"You can't just walk up all confident when you're totally not," Riya pressed, hustling to keep up.

"Yes, I can. And no—we don't need a plan." Haley didn't even slow down.

Her eyes locked ahead, every step sharp and certain.

"Grandma Ama said—once you pick a side, you're stuck."

"Okay, commander in leather and rage," Riya muttered—half joke, half nervous crack. "But without a plan, we're toast."

Her throat scraped raw as she swallowed. "I mean, look at us—we're the world's saddest Renaissance fair. Our 'army' looks like it crawled out of a cursed compost heap. And them?" She jabbed a shaky hand toward the ridge. "They're marching like celestial royalty."

Then, before Riya could blink, Haley's hand clamped down on hers—calm, unyielding, too strong.

"No more waiting," she said, her grip alive with purpose... and something hungrier.

Together, hand in hand, the cousins walked forward—right into what might become their greatest downfall.

CHAPTER FIFTY-SEVEN

HALLOWEEN

Through the setting haze, a figure emerged—tall and ageless, older perhaps than mercy itself, yet bearing the kind of youth that made time seem like a rumor.

The air bowed around her, trembling with the wild danger and unshakable calm that burned in her golden eyes. Plum hair streaked with solar gold spilled over an ivory face—still as a lioness before the strike.

"I am Zenox," she said, her voice carrying the weight of a thousand winters and the burn of a midsummer sun. "I am the keeper of Time's chains. Breaker of every bond. Cross me, and I'll rewrite you so completely it will be as if you never lived."

Behind her, the entire Light Veil dropped to one knee in perfect unison—then rose like a single breath.

"Your Light Oath reached us—and we've brought five hundred thousand Warriors to end Queen Hexima's reign."

Haley's pulse thundered, quick and wild, like hooves pounding the earth. *Rebuilder of timelines.*

She straightened her spine, forcing herself to meet the gaze of celestial royalty who would sooner see her ash than stand at her side.

"Zenox," she said, her voice steady, "thank you for answering our call. Your support means—"

"Yes... I am certain it does," Zenox said, each word measured—cool and sharp as shattered crystal. "Then tell me... why do Maldrops stand beside you?"

"They're no longer Maldrops," she said, voice low but carrying, each word steady as stone. "They took the Light Oath—and if that's a problem, you'll have to deal with me first."

Riya tugged at her sleeve, whispering in a rush.

"Haley, please don't piss off the one person who could *blink* her yellow eyes and retroactively delete our birth certificates."

Zenox stepped forward—every movement regal, every step a quiet threat. She lifted her shield with finality.

"We will not fight beside the Shadow Veil."

The murmurs behind her grew teeth, snapping through the crowd like a pack of wolves.

The air ripped open with a *crack*.

A roar tore across the field, low and guttural.

With a single sweep, Harshmoon moved—swift and soundless—appearing beside Zenox like the shadow of a jaguar slipping through midnight.

He seized her blade. For a breath, she yanked a dagger from her ankle, ready to take his arm clean off—

But then he did something she didn't expect.

Shwick.

He dragged the blade across his own palm.

Blood spilled. It struck the earth with a hiss.

And there it was—thick, glistening aqua blood coursed down Harshmoon's marble-cut arm, luminous as if the ocean itself had been bottled and spilled.

Zenox stilled, her gaze narrowing as if beholding a prophecy gone wrong.

"You bleed..." she whispered, the words catching in her throat, almost reverent. "Not the tar of Shadow. Not the rot of Everbind. Not Dahmorte's decay. But you bleed Light—pure, unbroken... whole. A blood that belongs only to the Hive. And yet..."

Harshmoon stepped toward her, slow and careful, like the ground might shatter beneath him.

"We beg thy pardon," he murmured, voice bowed low beneath its own weight. "Stand with us... my radiant Majestrix of Time."

Behind her, the Light Veil army swayed—an almost imperceptible ripple through perfect ranks.

The flawless wall of gold and silver frayed, edges unraveling like silk in a storm.

And then—

A *crack* split the heavens.

Playtime was over.

The final word had arrived—shimmering in silver, wrapped in a pantsuit.

CHAPTER FIFTY-EIGHT

HALLOWEEN

Queen Zion descended—white suit blazing, arms wide, skin glowing with the fire of ancient stars.

A single beam of light circled her spiraled hair like a living halo.

No crown was needed. She was one.

"I have watched the Lightwices bind what no one else dared touch," she said, her voice a bell of truth and thunder. "They stitched realms severed for centuries. They brought the impossible to its knees."

Then she turned—slowly, deliberately—to Zenox, her gaze as old as creation itself.

"But what I have yet to behold," she said, each word measured, "is trust."

Zenox lifted her shield. "We sought only to protect—"

"Silence!" Zion's voice split the air like a spear of light through stone. "The Veil has no sovereignty now. We are threads in the tapestry of the Fates— none above, none apart."

The force of it slammed into Riya's chest, leaving her ears ringing. For a beat, she just blinked, stunned. She leaned closer to Haley, voice bone-dry.

"Cool, cool, cool. Totally not terrifying at all. Definitely didn't just pee a little."

"Classy."

Riya's mouth twitched. "Everyone needs a legacy."

Zion's voice gentled, though it still carried the weight of ages. "If your hand cannot lift beside ours... then lay it down and depart."

Zenox's breath hitched. Her eyes searched Zion's face as if it were a map to some untold future. Her fingers trembled against the rim of her shield.

For a moment, she looked ready to run—or shatter. Then she nodded. Once.

"Beside you, we shall fight," Zenox said, her tone trembling with the weight of nightfall's first breath.

Queen Zion advanced, radiant and unshaken, her very presence bending the air.

She raised her hands—slow, deliberate—and the Veils behind her cinched closed in a single burst of searing light.

"Tonight," Zion proclaimed, her voice carrying wisdom and memory, "we stand as one. We strike as one. And we end this as one."

She raised her voice to the night sky.

"Victory is ours!"

The cheers rose—loud, wild, unstoppable. Like thunder waking the world.

Hooves pounded. Wings flared. Claws scraped.

For the first time, the Fates stood united.

And the cousins? Ready or not, they had forged a new universe— unshakable, unbreakable—because they made it together.

Because it was theirs.

CHAPTER FIFTY-NINE

HALLOWEEN

Aside from the raging battle unfolding just behind the cousins' houses—one only they could see—the neighborhood remained blissfully unaware.

Kids laughed through the streets in plastic fangs and glittery wings, dragging sacks of candy behind them.

Parents sipped cider, snapped photos, and admired gory lawn displays.

If they had looked *just a little harder*, past the smoke and shimmer in the air, they might have seen the truth.

A war was bleeding through the Veil. Hexima's army appeared like wasps swarming a turkey leg left to rot in the sun.

Over the dark ridge they came, pouring down as soon as the last light bled out of the sky—the true Maldrops, countless, unending.

Limbs contorted, snapping into place at impossible angles, as if each creature had forgotten how to walk and was relearning with every jagged step.

Jet-black warhorses thundered through the dark, their shoulders bristling with spears like the spines of a night-born sea monster. Frost poured from their nostrils in ghostly plumes, icing the cheeks of skull-helmed riders.

Mouths yawned open where no mouths should exist, gaping with wet, soundless hunger.

Eyes—if they could be called eyes—burned with a sick violet fire, a flame that rotted the trees themselves.

It was every horror film Riya had ever half-watched through her fingers, all mashed into one. Her wit failed her, and she did the only sensible thing.

"RUN!" she screamed. "Haley!"

275

But Haley didn't move.

She clamped down on Riya's arm with the grip of a lost puppy gone feral—unyielding, refusing to let her out of reach.

"Uh, death grip? Maybe let up?!" she spat. "Kinda need this arm free to protect Inky, remember? Grandma's last command?"

Haley didn't flinch. Her gaze was locked on the dark tide rolling closer, her entire mind and body pulled taut, every ounce of her bent toward the battle ahead.

The death toll was climbing. Steadily. Brutally.

And somewhere in that rising count, Haley knew—Hexima's shriveled excuse of a heart was waiting. When the Athame found it, she'd mount that raisin on a wall.

If Hexima wanted a war, Haley was ready to deliver.

And then—the sky broke.

Rain hammered down in meatloaf-sized drops—thick, relentless, pounding the battlefield until mud and blood ran together in choking rivers.

It didn't stop the violence. Nothing did. Solar flares cracked through the clouds. Fikas. Onuks. Blades made of moonlight.

Still, Hexima's Maldrops wouldn't stay down. Slice them. Burn them. Dismember them.

They squelched back together like evil sculpted clay, reforming in grotesque bursts, and came skittering—fast, twitchy—like spiders on pure adrenaline, every motion jerking toward the Light Warriors.

Even the headless kept swinging their swords, blades whistling through the air. Then the severed heads sprouted slick, insect-like legs and went scuttling after ankles, teeth snapping with wet, eager clicks.

Only a lucky few stayed dead—hit them just behind the ear, and they erupted in fire, collapsing into licorice-slick goo that sizzled as it hit the mud.

Then—

A Maldrop's head went sailing past the cousins like a cannonball—only to sprout legs mid-air and start chomping its way back, teeth first, right at Riya.

"No, no, nope," she said, choking back a scream. "Not today!"

The Lumex sagged in her grip, heavier than it should've been—and Riya wasn't even sure it worked on something made of pure undead nightmare fuel.

Haley, though, already had a plan.

The Athame tore free, comet-green light flaring as it split the beast's skull and buried itself in the grass, sizzling like spilled gasoline.

Riya gaped. "Are you crazy?!" She smacked Haley's arm.

"What?" Haley's tone was maddeningly calm. "It's my birthday, and I'll stab if I want to."

It was their birthday—shared down to the minute.

Back home, their classmates should've been trickling into Haley's house for cupcakes and chaos, but no one had even noticed they were gone.

No one wondered why the birthday girls were missing.

Haley smiled anyway.

Not for cake or confetti. For the simple fact that the Athame had chosen her. With every strike, it felt increasingly like a humble yet dangerous friend—the best kind.

A *whip-snap* of wind came from behind.

Zion stepped between them.

"Riya is correct, dear Haley," Queen Zion said, her voice crisp and edged with finality. "You must stay safe. I will not have either of you running off to your deaths."

A soft *pop* of green smoke—then suddenly, the cousins were suspended inside a levitating bubble. It shimmered like oil slicking across glass, swirling with faint whispers of light.

"You're invisible now," Zion added, dusting her hands. "No funny business." Her gaze locked on Haley like a spell in progress.

Haley crossed her arms, sulking in her floating trap.

She blew out a breath. "Great," she muttered. "A birthday-timeout-bubble."

Riya, however, cracked her first smile. "Weee!" she giggled, spinning like a kid on a jungle gym. She landed dramatically on Haley's shoulders with a theatrical curtsy.

Haley groaned and swam to the other side. "This is so dumb. We can't fight or help from in here."

"Exactly!" Riya beamed.

"That's what I need to talk to you about," Haley said, her tone dropping, sharp and steady. "Hexima has to die. It's the only way to break the curse—to save the Fates... and our souls from an eternity of Hexima-brand damnation."

Riya went rigid. Her skin flushed green—an actual shade of panic.

She had been so focused on keeping Inky safe that she spaced on breaking Hexima's curse—or *any* curse—the most apparent thing had slipped right through the cracks in her logic-riddled mind.

"But she's basically unkillable!" she blurted, her hands flying up as if she could somehow ward off reality with air quotes.

Haley, calm as ever, flicked a finger against her armor. *Clink.*

"My dad's Aza," she said flatly. "Yeah, that weapon—the one under my house. The creepy majick dungeon? It'll kill her."

Riya opened her mouth, ready to argue—to beg, maybe—to say

something that might pull Haley back from this insane and new plan.

But then she froze. Something had shifted. A flicker at the edge of her vision. A ripple in the air.

Her voice dropped to a whisper.

"Um... Haley."

She pointed, eyes wide.

"L-look."

And there she was.

Queen Hexima emerged in all her nightmare glory—crown of bone, cheeks sharp as a hexed blade—but something was wrong. Terribly wrong.

This time, she didn't just come alone.

She came with an army—over one million more Maldrops—marching at her curled boots like a living plague.

CHAPTER SIXTY

HALLOWEEN

Strutting into view like she owned the apocalypse, and flanked by her full-blown dumpster-goblin army, Hexima smiled—a sharp, gleaming thing, like a row of knives.

She leapfrogged across the egg-shaped heads of her army, cloak snapping like a whip, scepter swinging like a bat.

Then—sudden, sharp—she landed before Queen Zion, like a vulture slamming down to claim its kill.

Her neck twisted at an impossible angle, and Riya finally understood the nightmare truth of being double-jointed.

"WHERE," she roared, "are those little maggot witches, Zion?!"

She galloped on all fours, snarling and twitching, sniffing leaves, trees, shadows—muttering nonsense.

The bubble held. She couldn't sense the cousins.

But she knew. *She knew.*

"I know you're hiding them!" she hissed, fangs glinting as she hoisted a gremlin by the neck—its chest impaled by a rusted fish hook. The creature writhed and giggled.

"Give them to me," she spat, each word dripping venom, "or I'll let loose the Snatcher—and it will not rest until it has gnawed the marrow from your onu."

She flung it. The gremlin launched—claws splayed, eyes rabid—

Zion lifted one hand.

ZAP.

A spear of light ripped down from the heavens, pinning the creature to a tree before it burst into a cloud of dust.

In the same breath, Zion pivoted—her second strike snapping across the air and catching Hexima full in the face.

The impact carved a crater into her cheek, burning right through the glamor and rot.

Hexima reeled back, shrieking.

"ERGH!" she howled. "Enough games! Where are the impotent witches?!"

Zion stood firm.

Hexima's fury boiled over.

"Very well," she spat. "I'll kill you and find them myself."

Then—insanely—Hexima ripped the hair from her own scalp in one sickening tear, peeling it off like a wet sweater.

Riya recoiled. "Wait. *WHAT*? Why is her hair moving?!"

Hexima hurled it forward, and midair it writhed—black, wormy curls convulsing as veins split and teeth sprouted where strands should've been.

They lunged for Zion, a starving nest of serpents made from her own flesh, shrieking as they reached for her throat.

Riya gagged. "And it's an *assassin*?! Seriously—does everything on Hexima, glued down or otherwise, try to kill you?!"

Haley's grip cinched around the Athame.

"Yeah," she muttered, pulse hammering. "Definitely a bad hair day."

Zion didn't flinch.

She snatched Hexima's snarling hair mid-lunge, trapping it in a hovering orb of fire—then crushed it to vapor, scattering the ashes into mist.

A stench hit next—burnt silk mixed with rancid perfume—so strong Riya gagged and slapped a hand over her mouth.

Hexima clutched her scalp and shrieked, "MY HAIR!"

Zion casually dusted off her sparkling jacket, unfazed by the attack. Her voice rang out, crisp and ancient, as if it had been pulled up from Middle-earth.

"You call on old majick—Witch's Ladder. *Catch me once, catch me twice... bind thy cursed hair in a death-vice.*"

She stepped forward, light radiating from the deep-set hollows of her eyes.

"You've bled yourself dry tonight, Hexima—spilling what little power you had on a child's tantrum of a hex. And you know it. I'd be shocked if you could claw your way out of the wreck you've made."

Hexima's fingers curled over her now-bald scalp, nails digging into skin as her jaw trembled with rage.

Then from the fog, shapes began to emerge—slow, limping, wrong.

Riya recognized them instantly—not by their faces, but by the scraps of pink fabric and heels clinging to whatever was left.

CHAPTER SIXTY-ONE

HALLOWEEN

Audrey. Sarah. Staggered into view.

Their smiles were gone, peeled away into slack, gray skin stretched too thin.

Audrey's ears were nothing but torn holes; her jaw dangled loose, like a broken chicken bone, swinging with every garbled sound.

Beside her, Sarah's skin hung in strips, sagging off her frame like soaked paper dolls left too long in the rain—patches of rot peeling to reveal the gray bone beneath.

Behind the undead sisters came more—an entire crowd of familiar faces, festering shadow at Hexima's back.

Without a word, Zion hurled a fireball. It cut through the air in a perfect arc—and blew Audrey's arm clean off.

"W-witch!" Audrey screamed, clutching her smoking stump.

Zion didn't blink.

"I was merely informing your bald overlord that you and your swamp-born horde may crawl back to the mire that first spat you forth."

A flash of light exploded nearby, and a Malum lunged right for Zion—its jaw unhinged, dripping oil.

Haley's vision tunneled. Her senses fuzzed into static. She clenched her fist.

"Kill the Malums," Haley whispered to the Athame, her voice barely audible over the thunder.

The blade pulsed once—then launched itself into the fray like a streak of green lightning. It drove straight through the creature's skull.

The cursed blade whipped back toward Haley—but the instant it hit the bubble, a shockwave shattered it like candied glass, dissolving into a thousand shrieks of light.

Across the field, Hexima perked up. She clapped her hands like a deranged toddler at a birthday party.

"Aww, exposed—finally!" she cooed. "Just the way I like my next meal."

One of her molars plunked out mid-sentence, bouncing off her bony knee. "Time to die, witches!" she screeched.

Before the cousins could react, she raised her claws and chanted:

> *Like a dog with a scent*
> *Your days are spent*
> *I will always find thee*
> *No more hiding from me!*

Matching purple collars snapped around the cousins' necks with a sound like cracking bone. A heartbeat later, Hexima yanked. Invisible leashes snapped tight.

Zion lunged, light exploding from her palms—

But the moment her power touched the air, a lilac cage erupted from the earth, jagged and alive, snapping shut around her like a claw.

Hexima's grin spread—slow and predatory.

"I warned you," she purred, voice curling like blood around a blade. "I do not lose. I devour."

Hexima yanked the chains, and the cousins hit the ground hard at the Malums' moldy feet.

Riya didn't hesitate. She lifted the Lumex high.

Hexima's screeching cackle split the night.

"You think your little toy frightens me?" she spat, her smile cracked and gleaming. "I was forging darkness before your bloodlines even had names."

Audrey snorted, the sound gurgling through torn cartilage.

"Awww... wiii'tchesss... waaaan'... plaaayy..."

Sarah giggled, a wet rattle, her eyeballs jiggling loose with each shake.

"Yer... wii'ttle... babbyyy... weeep'onnsss... hows'... cuuutee..."

Riya gagged, eyes watering. "Oh wow... the stench—"

She stumbled back, then blurted, "T-Take this, y-you weirdos!" and gave the Lumex's beak a frantic rub, as if she were trying to wake a grumpy parrot.

Gray smoke exploded outward.

"Youuuuu stoopiddd witchhhhah!" Audrey yelled—but her voice

286

softened into baby coos.

Riya blinked.

"Wait... did she just sound like a newborn?"

All the Malums cried, cooed, and blew spit bubbles through their cracked, crusty lips.

"I hatteee babbbiesssss...!" Sarah screeched, then tripped over her own rotten foot.

Riya squinted.

"Wait... zombies are scared of babies?"

Haley blinked, her brows scrunching.

"Weird... but kind of perfect," she muttered, as if the universe had finally lost its mind in just the right way.

Riya stepped forward, her grip tightening on the Lumex.

"We have to do something," she said, her voice steady this time. "Zion's trapped... and sarcasm isn't cutting it anymore."

"Then we do something new," Haley said, flashing a grin that belonged on someone far more unhinged.

Ending this war in one strike? That temptation burned hotter than fear.

"Remember when Zion said going back in time gave us extra minutes?"

Riya squinted. "Yeah... so?"

She froze mid-blink.

"No. Naw. Nope. What brilliant, probably-fatal scheme have you been marinating in now?"

Haley paused. Then, with more confidence than she'd shown in twenty-four hours, she laid it out—curse-bending, death-defying, full Haley-style.

"Okay. I use my Zeno power, jump back to when I kinda died in the gloaming, and cash in the time Zion gave us," she said, voice steady now.

She swallowed, hearing how insane—and weirdly scientific—it sounded.

"Then I astral project, step out of my body. You stab me—like hitting the shell, not the *me*. That breaks the curse." She sliced a hand across her chest for emphasis.

"While I'm out, I grab the Aza. You heal me. Then—poof." She smirked, reckless and sure. "I come back, blast Hexima, and end this. For good."

Riya's mouth opened. Closed. Opened again. She looked like a startled nettle toad mid–fly chase—half outrage, half confusion.

She scrambled for something to say—something smart, something safe, something that wasn't, *"Sure, let me murder you real quick."*

She gathered her words, but when they finally broke free, they landed wrong—cold, sharp, nothing like what she meant.

"Not going to happen," she muttered, wincing. "This me-killing-you thing? Hard pass."

She twisted in place, turned the words over in her mouth a few times, then blurted—

"The only plan we should be focused on is protecting Inky—!"

Riya blinked, her chest heaving.

"I'm sorry—but no. Absolutely not."

Haley just shrugged, casual as ever, as if she were deciding on a snack, not a soul-splitting, magical death plan.

"We need to do this," she said, her voice like flint striking steel. "We fight fire with fire. And I'll burn it all down if that's what it takes."

Then she turned to Riya, eyes blazing with a new, unnerving fire.

"Your job? Make sure there's someone left to heal after I'm done."

CHAPTER SIXTY-ONE

HALLOWEEN

The Lumex pulsed—then drew in the cursed smoke as if it were breathing in a miniature storm.

The Malums collapsed—flattened like paper dolls under an avalanche of unseen hands. Silence followed, thick and humming with static.

Riya stepped through the haze, hand planted on her hip, glowing faintly from residual majick.

"What's wrong?" she called, her voice loud and clear. "Afraid of our *little* toys?"

Hexima snarled. Her voice curled through the air, low and coiled with malice.

"You know what must be done," she hissed. "One of you must kill the other."

Haley raised the Athame, grip steady.

"We understand the curse and—"

"Yes... Yes... yesss," came Hexima's hiss, low and lingering. "I tire of this illusion of valor you cling to, little one."

Maggots spilled from between her teeth, writhing over cracked lips as if they'd made a home there for centuries.

"One of you ends tonight. Let's see who screams the prettiest."

Riya trembled.

The plan—*the barely-held-together, probably-doomed plan*—was the only thing keeping her upright.

She turned to Haley with the path still fresh in her mind.

Dahmorte and Everbind had fallen—just like Haley predicted. Their army had grown with Hexima's castoffs and traitors.

The battle was shifting.

Fast.

Again—just like Haley predicted.

And next on the list?

Haley was supposed to use her Astroprojection powers—leave her body—so Riya could... stab her. Then, somehow, Haley would take care of the rest... Right.

Riya's voice shook, but she forced out the words in their secret language—the one no curse could twist:

"Era uoy ydear, Yaleh?"

Are you ready, Haley?

Haley nodded once. No smile. No tears. Just steel.

Then, without a word, she pointed to the shaped blade, the Onuk, strapped against Riya's leg like a promise neither of them wanted to keep.

Twin blades infused with fate-thread. Capable of slicing through spells, oaths, curses, and even time... at a cost.

Riya's heart dropped.

If she hesitated just long enough, it could all fall apart on its own. Maybe she wouldn't have to stab her cousin and hope she could bring her back.

Because that part? That was guesswork. Desperate, magical guesswork.

And Riya hated that—she needed steps. Clear ones. Concrete. Labeled.

But before she could protest, Haley's eyes fluttered shut.

She pictured herself back in the gloaming—that endless fall where time unraveled and eternity yawned wide.

Then, in the next breath, she imagined herself beneath the house, in the dark, where the air smelled of rust and dusty secrets. Her fingers curled in her mind around the Aza's cold steel—solid, silent, waiting.

Her limbs jerked, robotic and stiff, like her joints had run dry. The Astroprojection worked.

She felt it immediately—her soul peeled from her body like smoke under glass.

The world around her slowed, muffled, like she was watching everything from behind a thick plastic bubble.

But she didn't waste a second. Haley reached down, chaos in her steps, and unhooked the blade from Riya's belt—hands moving fast, breath held tight.

Riya flinched.

"No... H–Ha–ley," she whispered, her voice splintering.

Her hands trembled like live wires as she looked down, lips quivering.

292

Tears spilled freely now. She didn't bother wiping them away.

Her best friend. Her cousin. Her person. Her everything. The one who knew her secrets before she knew them herself. She couldn't lose her.

Hexima cut through the moment with a shriek. "What's taking so long? STAB HER!"

Haley gently wrapped Riya's trembling fingers around the knife. Riya hiccupped a sob.

"Splendid!" Hexima squealed. "DO IT NOW!"

Haley steadied Riya's hand, her eyes ghost-white, lips frozen shut— already looking dead.

With Riya's trembling hands guiding her own, Haley pressed the blade to her chestplate—and drove it in.

The steel slid through with chilling ease.

A soft gasp slipped from her lips—half breath, half goodbye—as blood splattered across Riya's face like crimson paint.

Then Haley fell—slick with rain, still, silent.

CHAPTER SIXTY-TWO

HALLOWEEN

The world didn't stop. But Riya's did.

"Haley?" The name cracked out of her throat, more plea than word. Her cousin's body lay slack in her arms—slick with rain, streaked with blood, terrifyingly still.

For a second, there was no battle.

"No... no, no, no." The words tore out of her lungs, half prayer, half curse.

Hexima's laughter sliced the air—razor-thin, triumphant.

"One little witch falls... and the other will surely follow."

She tore free of her invisible perch like a deranged bat unspooled from the dark, her bald head blistering beneath a crown of purple fire, skin bubbling like grilled cheese as the flames ate across her scalp.

She tugged at the folds of her neck—wrinkled and slick, like boiled hot dogs left too long in water—and hissed, "I may yet claim the sum of your powers." Her words oozed slow, deliberate. "Your onus remains... untouched. For now."

Riya's heart bottomed out.

"But—we broke your curse!" she stammered, the words splintering on her tongue. "I... I killed her. I did."

Hexima laughed, the sound brittle and cruel, like glass shattering against bone.

"You broke a curse—though not mine in full." Her eyes gleamed with rot.

"What do you mean—the curse is not totally your?" Riya shot back.

Hexima's jaw sagged open—hingeless, obscene—her tongue swaying in the air like a fishhook.

"Oh, look at you catching on, little witch," she crooned. "Did you finally sniff out the lie?"

Her smile split wider, skin straining at the seams.

"That curse you cracked?" She hissed. "Only half mine. The rest..." Her gaze slid like a blade toward Riya. "The rest belongs to your fathers. A poisoned heirloom—misfortune passed like a leash. One you've worn gladly, stumbling blind in the dark."

Then—

SNAP.

Hexima's palms slapped flat. A sphere of violet lightning cracked alive between them—humming, snarling, writhing.

BOOM.

The blast punched through Riya's chestplate. She shot backward, her armor sparking, her body whipping like a rag doll.

Riya's vision blurred. But she didn't pass out. She couldn't. Haley needed her.

Muscle memory fired. Varsity tennis. Sophomore year.

No time to think.

Riya seized the severed head of a Maldrop—its three twitching tongues dangling like overcooked spaghetti.

She spotted a discarded shield, planted her feet, and served it like a tennis champ from hell.

Wham.

The skull whirled through the air—teeth bared, spinning like a cursed discus. It slammed Hexima square in the throat.

CHOMP.

Hexima screeched, clawing at her throat like she was swatting a ten-pound wasp made of pure rage.

Riya smirked.

"One-love."

No time to gloat. She bolted—mud flying, heart pounding—straight for Haley.

But something was wrong. Haley's arms, legs, neck... shriveled.

As if she were collapsing in on herself. Like time had turned her into some deflating roadkill lizard—shrinking, caving, unraveling.

Riya gasped. Hexima must've done something.

WHACK.

A flash of ghostly lavender—then blinding pain ripped through the back of Riya's skull. White stars burst behind her eyes. She staggered, the world tilting sideways.

Hexima dropped to all fours, snarling. The Maldrop's head was still clamped to her shoulder like a grotesque brooch.

"I've hunted you since your first breath," she murmured, her voice sharp and cold. "Now it's time to die."

Somewhere behind Hexima, deep in the dark, something massive shifted—slow, deliberate—like the sound of a tomb unlocking itself.

Then—she charged.

CHAPTER SIXTY-THREE

HALLOWEEN

Finally, Haley thought.

She'd fallen through endless darkness and landed somewhere new—somewhere far from the battlefield.

For once, something had actually gone her way. Her astral projection had worked.

Too bad she'd crash-landed in her own closet.

"Really?" Haley groaned, brushing phantom dust off her shirt. "I survive death just to mess up my first spell?"

She smacked her forehead, her hand passing right through before reforming. "Seriously. Is there, like, a tutorial for this?"

When she lifted her head, the world had changed. Color was gone—bled out—leaving only shades of black and white, smeared into endless gray.

She stepped out of the closet—only for her foot to snag on something unseen. She didn't know what it was. She only *knew*.

The way a child knows not to grab a hot pan or test a candle flame with bare fingers.

A ribbon of cooled lightning, threading through the floorboards like the house had veins. It whispered.

Stay. Fall. Rest. Cross my depths, and never again shall you wear the flesh that bore you.

Shapes flickered in its depths, drifting like paper lanterns underwater.

Their faces were warped, mouths open in silent ovals, eyes wide with the kind of peace that never ended.

Haley jumped—ungraceful as ever—and toppled over the glowing stream like she was flunking gym class.

"Ten out of ten," she deadpanned to no one. "Would definitely haunt myself again."

She winced, glancing over her shoulder. "Round two?" she muttered, like a half-baked spell. "Basement this time."

Reality stuttered—then tilted.

She landed hard, skidding across damp stone. A single light glimmered in the dark—dim, flickering, definitely wrong.

Haley drifted forward, ghost-hands twitching, phantom boots stumbling against nothing.

And then—there it was.

The Aza.

Set in its clearing like a diamond under glass, gleaming as though the whole house had been built just to display it.

Then—*sniff.*

It hit her like a slap. Wet dog. Dipped in dead fish.   Haley gagged. *Great. Ghost nose works fine, but ghost vision's in grayscale mode? Thanks for nothing, afterlife manual.*

She edged forward—more wobble than grace—then froze.

Sniff. Sniff. *Sniff.*

Then—*swap.*

Something big shifted in the shadows, brushing against the haze like it owned the place.

"...A Shiverskin?" Haley whispered. "How did it get down here?"

The creature's nostrils flared—once. Twice.

Then it roared—a sound like rusted metal tearing apart—and lunged.

Claws whipped through the air in a frenzy, slicing wild and unhinged, like a blind squirrel armed with knives and nothing to lose.

Haley's fists curled. Her palms snapped together—

CRACK.

A shockwave ripped free.

The wave slithered forward like a snake skimming the surface of water, ripples spiraling in its wake. But it was the color that made Haley's stomach knot.

Purple. Deep purple. Like a bruise that wouldn't stop bleeding.

Shadow magic.

It hadn't asked. It hadn't waited. It tore out of her like instinct. Like breath.

Was this what Hexima felt? The rush? The hunger? The ease?

And that's what scared her most.

Unlike Riya, Haley hadn't learned how to dance with her Shadow without losing herself.

Every time she touched it, it whispered in Hexima's voice—mangy, twisted, feral.

But now it had chosen the strike. An onuk blade sang once through the dark—and the Shiverskin's head toppled free, hitting the ground with a wet, hollow thud.

Its body jittered, arms flailing before it collapsed in a heap of fur and bone. Black tar fanned across the floor, slick and smoking where it touched the stone.

Haley staggered back, her breath stuttering.

The mist still curled around the blade, cradling it, stroking it like a prize.

The air thickened—clotted and sour, like milk left out too long.

There—half-buried in stone—was the Aza. Haley's fingers brushed it.

WHOOSH.

BOOM.

She slammed back into her dead body.

But what should have been the end of Hexima and her Maldrop army... was only the beginning of the end for Haley and Riya.

CHAPTER SIXTY-FOUR

HALLOWEEN

Back on the battlefield, amid the clash of metal and the crack of breaking bones, Haley's body bounced like a robotic bunny.

Riya didn't know much about astral projection, but she was pretty sure the dead weren't supposed to jolt three feet into the air.

And if Haley was back—where was the Aza?

The revolver. Ancient. Deadly.

Built to fire three bullets in a single, perfect chord. The only weapon sharp enough, final enough, to kill Hexima, break the curse, and save the Fates.

But there was no gun. No chance. Riya's chest hollowed.

Hexima coiled for another strike—then was slammed aside by a burst of raining fire.

Diving from the sky like a winged shadow, Tayka's ears flared wide, her hands blazing with silver flame.

Inside the glass cockpit—faces pressed to the windows—were the cousins' family. Exhausted. Wide-eyed. Glowing just faintly with the trace of majick they'd sworn not to use.

A trumpet of fire bursts chased Hexima through the waxy knolls and twisted shadows, lighting up her retreat like a cursed firework show.

She hissed, ducking behind a crumbling mound of bones as another blast sizzled past her cheek, singeing the air.

Then—

"Die, you twitchy bat fiend!" Hexima shrieked.

From her mangled palms, a lavender electrical storm erupted—howling

303

like a hurricane made of knives.

It screamed across the battlefield, slamming into Tayka's ship before anyone could breathe.

BOOOOM.

The sky didn't just split—it tore.

The Fuka shuddered, its frame groaning like a dying beast. Metal turned to meteors. Flames to falling stars.

Riya and Haley's family were trapped inside. Before Riya could even scream, the ship crumpled—twisted into a mess of burning paperclips.

It felt impossible. After everything they'd survived, Hexima had delivered a blow so final it made Riya wish she were as gone as Haley.

Her hands trembled. "Ha—ley... ple—ase."

She collapsed beside her cousin's crumpled form, her voice splintering into jagged shards.

"Mom, Dad... everyone... gone... You have to come back. Please."

Riya clapped her hands to summon an eerie tan mist—like some haunted racecar zooming through the air—but it only made Haley look more like a crumpled bag of chips.

Swallowing her frustration, she dropped to her knees and moved her hands over Haley's chest.

"Why did I think I could do this?" Riya whispered, hands trembling. "I'm not some healer—I can't even bring a fish stick back to life, let alone you."

The gap between what she knew and what she needed to know wasn't just big—it was cosmic, like trying to cross a canyon on a spaghetti noodle, cosmic.

With trembling fingers, Riya pressed her hands to Haley's heart one last time, whispering words she didn't fully understand.

Beneath her palms—nothing.

Then... a stutter.

A single, weak thud, like a drumbeat too far away to hear. Her own heart skipped—then fell into rhythm with it, almost against her will.

Thud... hers.

Thud... Haley's.

A flicker of green lit under her fingers, faint as the first leaf in spring.

BOOM.

The world split open.

Light and sound roared outward in a shockwave, hurling her backward like a flower in a hurricane. She slammed into the ground, skidding through soot and dried blood.

Haley's limbs twitched. Her arms stretched. Her legs uncurled. She was filling back out—no longer shriveled, no longer fading.

304

But when her eyes snapped open—like a cursed doll's—something was wrong.

The honey-brown warmth was gone, replaced by two glowing eclipses, dark and impossible to look away from.

"Ha... ley..." Riya breathed, the name splintering as she scrambled back.

The change warped Haley's entire face. Her features, still familiar, had been rearranged by something demonic.

Riya's chest tightened like someone had cinched her ribs with wire. She stared at Haley—alive, maybe—but not right.

And then the memory slammed back.

Zion's voice, sharp as frostbite:

"Bring someone back for personal gain... and they might come back wrong."

Riya swallowed hard.

What if she hadn't saved Haley? What if she'd replaced her with something evil?

Riya's hands hovered inches from her cousin's arm, trembling.

And then—

POP.

The Aza blinked into existence, right in Haley's hand.

It didn't shimmer. It pulsed.

SNAP—Haley jolted upright, spine ramrod straight like someone yanked invisible strings.

"Ha... le... yyy?" Riya edged closer. "Are you...?"

Her cousin's eyes rolled back—just whites.

"That's a *no*."

No blink. No flinch.

Just those dead eyes like a smudge on a mirror.

The gun didn't shake—not even when Haley leveled it at Riya's temple.

This wasn't Haley.

Something else had come back wearing her skin.

And it was holding a loaded gun.

CHAPTER SIXTY-FIVE
HALLOWEEN

Riya, pale as a banana smoothie and twice as shaken, stared down the barrel of her biggest mistake.

Haley wasn't Haley. Not in the slightest.

She reached out, gently touched Haley's icy wrists, and nudged the revolver off course until it aimed at a charred tree stump.

"There you go, cowgirl," Riya whispered, voice trembling. "That's a better place for target practice... before Hexima makes another grand entrance."

Riya wished—no, *ached*—to trade powers with Haley. Just for a moment. Just long enough to undo this.

She'd rewind to three days ago—back to arguing over costumes and candy trades, not standing in the ruins of their world.

Then—

The stench hit first—sulfur and rot, like eggs left to stew in a burning dumpster.

The rumble swelled, bubbling from the dirt. The ground split open—and something green and slick launched out.

A frog.

Riya gagged, her whole body jerking.

"WHAT?!"

The frog landed with a soft *plop* in the mud.

Then, unbelievably, it waved—a casual little flick of its webbed hand like, *Hey girl*—before croaking,

"*Psst. Dearest Riya. It is I, Queen Zion.*"

Riya nearly blacked out.

"Zion?! As in—THE Queen Zion? In frog form?"

"Indeed."

Zion's voice steadied, resonant even through the croak.

"To steady the loom of the Fates, I placed a fragment of borrowed time in your hands. Haley bends that time now—shaping it with her Zeno gift. She is far more powerful than she believes."

Riya blinked hard. "Haley can barely skip recess without tripping. And now she's bending time?"

Zion flicked her tongue and snagged a passing gnat with disturbingly regal precision. She nodded, eyes wide and wise.

"Place your faith in your cousin. My form wanes... my breath thins. Take the Aza, child of light. Seal the work that must be done."

Then—

PERF.

Zion melted—like an expired marshmallow—oozing into a puddle of sticky, glowing green goo.

"UGH! Magical frog guts!" Riya gagged, dry-heaving into her elbow.

"I hate this. I *really* hate this!"

As the goop sizzled into the mud, doubt curled in her gut like a storm. Zeno magic? Haley?

Time-bending wasn't something you just... *winged*.

Haley might have had a gift for science—anything tangled in reality, space, or the kind of math that made Riya's eyes cross. Maybe she could pull this off—maybe more.

Still... Zion had said *Take the Aza.*

"Give it!" Riya snapped, hands out as Haley wobbled upright, limbs shaking like jelly.

Somehow—impossibly—Haley raised the Aza and leveled it at Hexima.

The witch stalked closer, every step a grotesque chorus of cracking joints and oozing laughter.

"How tragic," she cooed. "A corpse clutching the only weapon that can kill me."

Riya froze.

But then—she slid her fingers over Haley's—CRACK.

Haley's finger bent the wrong way.

Riya gasped.

Haley jolted, twitching like a shocked goat. Her head lolled.

The Aza gleamed in her corpse-like grip.

Hexima tilted her head, smiling with the sweetness of spoiled honey.

"Oh... can't do it, can you, Riya?" the voice purred. "Can't break what's been broken since your first breath? Tell me—can you rebuild anything?"

A low laugh rippled through the air, cold and deliberate.

"You are the reason your bloodline is ash. I turned your kin to glittering dust. And soon... your precious book will follow and kneel before—"

BANG. BANG. *BANG.*

Three bullets of ice-fire ripped from the Aza—light and death braided together.

But they stopped—caught by the one thing Riya had sworn to protect with her life.

And in that instant, her world unraveled—one mistake at a time.

CHAPTER SIXTY-SIX

HALLOWEEN

With a wet, slurping *gulp*, followed by a slow, almost satisfied *belch*, Inky blinked its one eye—then swallowed the bullets whole.

Like they were nothing. Like it had been forged for it, fated for it, since the dawn of majick.

Haley blinked. Her storm-black voids collapsed into warm, earthy brown. Gold shimmered across her dark, honey skin. She was back. Breathing. Alive.

But the victory lasted only a heartbeat. Hexima still lived—and she held Inky, fluttering like a confused bird before curling in on itself, paling, withering.

A wind swept in—not wind, but something colder. Hungrier. From the edges of the clearing, where the lavender moonlight refused to touch, came a sound.

Riya turned.

Audrey and Sarah stepped out from the shadows—if you could still call them that.

The zombie sisters hissed in stereo, drool stringing to the dirt.

Somewhere behind them, Hexima's laugh curled through the air like smoke.

"The Fates hunger for blood," she cackled, gliding behind Audrey and Sarah. "And it's yours they crave."

And then Haley... moved.

The world slowed to a nightmare crawl—every sound dragging, every breath an eternity.

Her mistakes cut through her mind like serrated knives: risks backfired, choices twisted into consequences she couldn't undo.

But this—this she could fix.

Kill the Malums.

Haley was the executioner. The heir to a new throne. She was Zeno.

"If the Fates want blood, they can have it—so long as it's yours!"

Then she lunged—Athame raised, palms outstretched.

A new surge sparked beneath her skin, and a violet storm followed—snapping, alive, like a wild, electric tail of ruin.

Behind Audrey and Sarah, the Veil of Dahmorte yawned open—an endless rift of Shadow and hunger.

Audrey shrieked.

"Waaait—wha' you doin'?" she slurred, one eye rolling. "We... don'... got our am'lets!" she wailed, palms jerking outward in a twitchy, half-defensive spasm. "We can'tttt cross! You'll... you'll rip ussss... dead-dead!"

Riya's breath caught—not from the Veil, but from Haley.

Her cousin stood in the Shadowlight like she'd been born to it, no fear, no hesitation—only raw, volcanic intent.

The only person Riya had ever seen tear open a portal like that was Queen Zion herself, a master among masters... and here was Haley, a novice, doing it with nothing but instinct and fury.

A part of her burned with awe. Another with something hotter—envy.

She'd always been the cautious one—the safety-first everything—triple-checking even her sandwich making, down to the millimeter of sliced deli meat.

But Haley?

Haley had no filters. No fear of the current that could consume her as easily as obey her—and that recklessness was turning her into something unstoppable.

Legendary, even.

Riya's chest tightened. If she couldn't learn to let that same wild force burn through her veins and master it, then all her careful control wouldn't save her. It would destroy her.

Either way, Riya felt it—the distance forming between them. The first of a thousand silent goodbyes.

Before she could catch her breath, Haley surged forward—a blur of vengeance and muscle.

Audrey and Sarah tumbled, limbs flailing, squashed like insects as they plunged into the Shadow Veil, sinking like stones in black water.

BOOM.

Their bodies burst in twin shocks of Shadow, rot and dust scattering in a halo of violet shrapnel.

But when the smoke cleared, ghostly shapes hovered where they'd fallen—perfect again. Unbroken.

Their skin luminous, hair as it once was, blonde and fine, eyes clear blue and alive.

Riya and Haley froze.

For a heartbeat, it seemed like Audrey and Sarah could be saved. But their souls didn't stay perfect for long.

Needle-like teeth unspooled from their gums, stringing down like wet yarn caught in a cat's claws. Their hair puffed into a damp, spongy crown fit for a nightmare clown.

Thousands of voices poured from the zombie sisters' throats—low, high, overlapping—Riya's own among them. Haley's too. Older. Angrier. Frayed with futures they hadn't lived yet.

One stays behind.
One slips into Shadow.
Both are bound.
Neither survives unbroken.

Haley's mouth barely twitched at the corners.
Destroy them.
Snap.
Green fire screamed from the Athame, ripping through ghost-flesh.
Whoosh.
Riya stepped beside Haley and let it all burst free—the rage, the sorrow, the loss.

All she'd ever wanted was a life filled with laughter, beauty... and Haley.

But the sisters, Hexima, and every pit-born monster in their orbit had stripped her clean of that—of everything.

Her Chemisource flared, uneven at first, jagged like rows of shark teeth. Then the waves steadied, heat flooding her veins, sparking at her fingertips.

The sisters' pig-like shrieks dissolved into static before their bodies convulsed—then crumpled into a writhing wisp of smoke.

And then—CRACK.

The Veil slammed shut—leaving only silence. Suffocating silence.

But it wasn't peace. Something was wrong.

Riya's heart stuttered.

"Wait... where is *she*?" The words barely scraped her throat.

Hexima—gone.

And with her... Inky.

Not even a whisper of magic left behind.

Only the cold certainty of sleight of hand.

Somewhere, beyond the Veils, an evil queen with the stolen Fates was already moving her pieces into place.

The real war had only just begun.

CHAPTER SIXTY-SEVEN

HALLOWEEN

For miles, nothing remained.

Hexima's Maldrop army had scorched everything into a molten smear. Shrubs. Rocks. Even the air shimmered like bruised flesh.

Riya's heart didn't know which command to follow—pound, break, or surrender.

"I failed everyone," Riya muttered. She tore the Lightwice seal from her chest—ripping it free like it burned.

"Riya!" Haley's voice cracked, not with anger, but something worse—betrayal.

She caught the seal midair, fingers curling around it like she could crush meaning back into it.

"You don't get to quit," Haley said, her voice steady, blade-sharp. "You didn't fail anything—or anyone. They failed you. All of them. It started with the cosmic-sized lies our families told... or worse, the truths they buried. And—"

Riya's eyes brimmed, her throat tight.

Haley had always been her biggest supporter, but in this moment, she didn't feel worthy of it.

"I haven't even told you the worst part," she rasped. "Speaking of family... Hexima let something slip. About our dads."

She spun, clutching Haley's arms to keep herself from walking away.

"She said—the curse, the one that made me kill you—it wasn't just hers. Half of it came from our dads. They built it, Hales. They decided we'd stay in

317

stormwinds.

"Riya speaks true," she thundered. "Do you deem this punishment just? Our charge is to hunt Queen Hexima—not cast these daughters into the maw of devouring!"

Zion stepped forward, her suit catching the purple moonlight.

"Yes, step back, Treewith," Zion said, her voice tolling like a bell. "Judgment is mine to bear. The Lightwices need no heavy hand—they are guided by the steadiest of hearts."

"Hush!" Ms. Treewith shrieked. "Shall I spell it out for you? Ms. Riya stabbed her cousin—killed her—then dragged her back! Tell me, does that not reek of personal gain?"

Riya's jaw dropped. "Are you for real right now? Haley's the one who did the whole deadly deed—she's the slayer here! I just hit restart so we could, you know, save the Fates and break the curse!"

Her gaze flicked to their fathers—sharp, skeptical— *We'll talk later.*

She turned back, lips curling. "Or did that slip your ancient, dust-choked mind?"

Ms. Treewith was not amused. She fluttered her thick, broken-licorice lashes like a cursed doll on its final blink.

"Then watch," she spat, her voice dropping low—sharp as broken glass. "And tell me these teenage wrecking balls don't deserve the Door of Bones."

She clapped her hands, but instead of majick, only a pitiful puff of dust drifted out.

"Hexima has drained us dry," she said, her voice flat with dread. "We march into a cursed world... powerless."

Her eyes snapped to the cousins.

"But their powers remain," she hissed, envy curling her words. "Go on—test them. Please," she mocked.

Zion gave a single nod. The signal was clear.

Riya lifted her hand. Power crawled over her knuckles like electrified inchworms—then a spark leapt free, slicing through a hissing tree.

Haley followed, breath sharp. She spun a Zeno spell, and time lurched forward—one day and three minutes. Still night. Still haunted.

Ms. Treewith clacked forward, stubby heels biting the ground. "See?" she crowed. "What did I predict? They can withstand the cursed new world."

And the curse had already begun.

Streetlamps spat shadows instead of light, crawling across the ground. The sky blinked, each star winking out one by one. In the distance, black fog slithered over rooftops, bowing shingles like prey under a predator's paw.

Zion advanced, her words steeped in the solemnity of ages long forgotten.

318

"Children of Lightwice," she intoned, "you must bind flame to Shadow. Even tainted, your powers endure. Hexima's mark clings to you—one that may seed salvation... or doom."

And just like that, it wasn't a war anymore.

It was a choice—chain the ones who might save the world... or lose them to the Shadow forever.

For the first time, Riya and Haley understood what real power meant.

Their magic was wide awake now—burning in the wrong corner of the universe.

To Riya, that meant caution.

To Haley, it meant doom if she dared another spell.

Failures aside, there was no escaping the truth: their fates were tangled with Hexima's, bound by a curse they couldn't yet undo.

And still—they had each other.

Riya's devotion to the Light.

Haley's instinct for the Shadow.

Two halves of something dangerously whole.

For all the universe's grandeur, it had never rested in more unforged—but undeniably brilliant—hands.

320

CHAPTER SIXTY-EIGHT

HALLOWEEN

The prophecy still thrummed in Riya's bones as she yanked Haley's wrist, dragging her out of the crowd—away from the Rede's fractured stares, away from their family's hollow relief at being spared the Door of Bones... for now.

They didn't get far.

A tree loomed ahead. Except it wasn't a tree anymore—its bark hardened to stone, its trunk coiled like a serpent.

Riya tried to ignore it, but a branch slithered up her arm.

"So... trees are snakes now. Cool. Totally normal."

Haley snorted, though her laugh cracked. "Right? Next thing you know, the swings at the playground will start hissing the alphabet."

Riya shot her a look. "Don't joke. You know they would."

Silence stretched, heavy with the hum still bleeding through the air.

Finally, Riya whispered, "Haley... what if this is permanent? What if this—" she gestured at the twisted bark, the warped sky, their family shouting off in the distance "—is our new normal?"

Haley's jaw tightened, but her voice held. "Then we survive it. Like we always do. With Fates, without Fates. Whatever."

Riya's chest cinched. "You make it sound so easy."

"It's not," Haley admitted, eyes glinting in the strange new light. "But if the universe thinks two Lightwices can't handle it—well... it hasn't been paying attention."

Riya's lips twitched into a reluctant grin. "Guess we'll just have to prove the Fates right. Or wrong. Or... something."

Haley bumped her shoulder. "Something sounds about right."

She slid her fingers through Riya's, steadying the shake.

"And by something, I mean we fight it. Together."

The wind picked up, dragging at their tangled hair. Above them, a shimmer cracked across the bruised sky like the universe exhaling.

Riya's mouth curved into a small, stubborn smile. "Maybe this isn't the end. Maybe it's just the start."

Haley squeezed her hand, eyes burning in the strange new light.

"Then maybe we were always meant to rewrite how it ends."

The purple-hazed moon washed the cousins' silhouettes in ghostlight, while behind them, frost crept silently over the trees.

It wasn't wind. It wasn't light. It was something older—something that slithered between breath and silence.

A whisper.

A hiss.

A curse, reborn.

From the air itself, parchment sparked—not with fire, but with malice. It floated weightless, its edges curling into black ash.

It lingered for a single heartbeat. Then vanished into the shadows, leaving one word behind—etched in silver flame:

RECKONING.

And somewhere far off, buried in the marrow of Hexima's newborn dominion... *The Book of Fates* did not whisper.

It laughed.

Cosmic Gratitude

Writing *The Book of Fates: As Darkness Rises* was like chasing stardust through a dream. This story wouldn't exist without the magic, love, and undying patience of so many.

To my family—

Thank you for believing in my whirlwind imagination, and my unlikely quest to find majick hidden inside the laws of physics. You never flinched when I insisted the universe could be both quantifiable and enchanted.

To my friends—

Thank you for letting me vanish into fictional worlds for hours (okay, years) and still texting me like I was normal.

To every teacher, librarian, and book-loving soul—

Whoever handed me a story that made me feel seen—This is me passing that light forward.

To my editors and early readers—

You took a tangle of shadowy metaphors and chaotic character arcs and helped turn them into something fierce and beautiful.

To my readers—

If you've ever felt out of place, too much, not enough, or like you might be holding secret powers inside you, you are the reason this story exists. Never stop chasing the truth in your soul, your onu.

And finally—To Inky. May your pages always find the right hands.

This is only the beginning.

www.ingramcontent.com/pod-product-compliance
Lightning Source LLC
Chambersburg PA
CBHW021453240626
47154CB00002B/350